That's What **Friends** Are For

That's What Friends Are For

a novel by JONI HILTON

Covenant Communications, Inc.

Published by Covenant Communications, Inc.
American Fork, Utah

Printed in the United States of America
First Printing: May 1997

04 03 02 01 00 99 98 97   10 9 8 7 6 5 4 3 2 1
ISBN 1-57734-111-2

Other Books by Joni Hilton:

As the Ward Turns
Around the Ward in 80 Days
Scrambled Home Evenings
Dating: No Guts, No Glory
Guilt-Free Motherhood
Honey on Hot Bread . . . and Other Heartfelt Wishes

Tapes by Joni Hilton:

As the Ward Turns
Around the Ward in 80 Days
Scrambled Home Evenings
Guilt-Free Motherhood, Parts 1 and 2
Dating: No Guts, No Glory
Caught in a Casserole
Coping with Male PMS
Woman Is that She Might Have Joy

For my husband and children,
whom I would choose as my friends,
and for my friends—Cynthia, Karen,
Christy, Teru, Nanette, and Deniece—
whom I would choose as my family.

It's funny how, in a matter of just sixty seconds, you can wreck your car, beat up a bank robber, find out who your friends are, and get free donuts for life.

Usually the life of a seventeen-year-old ticks along a little slower than that. But recently things stepped up a bit, and all because Courtney's mom has a job in the Mormon church.

Courtney is my best friend, and the best-looking girl at Jefferson High School. That's not why she's my best friend, of course. Under that slender, elegant exterior, Courtney is actually the only person who gets my jokes. She takes me seriously when I say my life-long dream is to become the world's greatest journalist, and she loves the stuff I write. She also comes to my rescue at times when I'm in trouble—which, like I say, have been picking up lately.

Her family is Latter-day Saint, which I'd never heard of before meeting Courtney. I've discovered several things about these Mormons. First, they're always going to something at their church—not just Sunday meetings, but parties and stuff. This is actually pretty cool; Courtney has invited me to some great dances and dinners. Second, Courtney's parents are strict and wouldn't let her date until she turned sixteen. This has come in extremely handy for me, since I do not share Courtney's dazzling appearance and have not yet been asked out on a date. (As a matter of fact, I borrowed this rule to pretend that's why *I* wasn't dating yet.)

Third, there's some kind of honor code or ethics they have, sort of an integrity thing, and I like that. As a future journalist, I plan to borrow once again from Courtney's family, and post all kinds of values and quotes on my desk in the newsroom. I'm sure there's more to their religion than that, but those are the things I've noticed so far.

Anyway, Courtney's mom needed the family wagon to haul scenery to their church for a musical they're putting on, and that left Courtney without any wheels on a day when she had an acting audition. Courtney has been modeling for years, and now she's trying to break into TV commercials. Naturally, I was happy to drive her there, because, just like Courtney believes in my dreams, I believe in hers.

I picked her up in my very own Mazda, a used and rebuilt car that purrs like a kitten, and which I have named Mazda-rati. My dad is a car mechanic, and came across it as a clunker with potential. After a few weeks with Dad, the car was reborn. Lucky me.

Courtney came running out of her house just as I bounced over the gutter and into her driveway. "I just noticed the audition is at four-thirty instead of five," she shouted, waving a map and throwing her purse into the back seat. "Gun it!"

Gun it? My baby, my Mazda-rati? At the first stoplight, I checked her map. Maybe there was a shortcut. Sure enough, we could bypass a boulevard with a million stoplights if we cut through some alleys a block away from the appointment.

Then, just as we arrived, just inches from the cross-street where her audition was, I slammed on the brakes. "What on earth—"

I stared across the street, where a man waving a gun was running out of a bank. Courtney followed my gaze and froze. There wasn't even time to gasp.

"My gosh—he just robbed that bank!" I shouted. And then, ever the ace reporter, I stepped on the gas to head him off, or get a good look at him, or do *something* besides just sit there in an alley. I mean, here was a story unfolding before my eyes.

"Are you crazy?" Courtney screamed, grabbing the gearshift and throwing it into reverse.

Bam! The back of the car slammed into a trash bin in the alley, which was still not as loud as Courtney yelling that we should get out of there.

And I, exhibiting the same brilliant judgment you see moths using near open flames, opened my door and ran toward the scene of the crime. Okay, so I am not as wise and mature as my Mormon friend—after all, she's had years of training or something. I did, however, have the sense to yell "Stay here!" to her as I ran off to cover the story.

At the end of the alley, I bumped full speed into the robber, who fell back and hit his head on a parking meter, then rolled to the ground, groaning. Suddenly Courtney was tackling me, knocking me to the sidewalk and lying on top of me. "Stay down!" she hissed. What on earth— was she this guy's accomplice?

"Get off me!" I yelled.

"No!" she roared back.

I turned my head and saw two policemen running over to us. "Get him!" I yelled to the policemen. "He just robbed that bank— get his gun!" What has happened to the world, I thought to myself, when a teenage girl has to shout instructions to officers of the law?

Now some other men were helping the robber to his feet, and one finally pulled Courtney off me, at which point I scrambled to my feet and thought about decking my former best buddy.

"Hey, girls," one of the men was saying, "we're shooting a commercial here—relax."

What? I looked like a freeze-frame on a home video of someone with their mouth wide open. The robber was rubbing his head, looking at us like we were idiots. And then, down the street, I saw the catering trucks, the cameras and lights, the snickering crew.

I brushed off my jacket and sneered at the man who appeared to be in charge. "Seems to me you could have posted some *signs* or something. You could give somebody a heart attack, you know."

"The main street is blocked off," he said, still smiling at my ridiculous assumption. "We don't usually post signs in alleys."

"Well, maybe you should," I snapped, so angry I was all but mimicking him. "They are open to the public, you know."

He nodded, still smiling. "Yes, I know."

I glanced back down the alley. "My car is wrecked, no thanks to you clowns."

Courtney cringed. I think I could be missing one of those brain filters that sift through what you're thinking before you actually say it.

"I'm terribly sorry about your car," the man said.

I glared at him. "C'mon, Courtney, let's get out of here."

"Umm . . ." Courtney was clearly humiliated. "I think this is where my audition is."

"Oh—you're here to tackle the dummy," the man said.

"How dare—" I began, but Courtney had clamped her hand over my mouth with lightning speed.

"It's an exercise equipment thing," she whispered, removing her hand. "Not you. It's the commercial I'm trying out for." And then, "As if I still have a chance."

"Sorry," I whispered back. "But look at my car, Courtney."

The man then introduced himself as the director of the commercial we had just interrupted—which, coincidentally, was being filmed just two doors from the casting office.

"My friend is a journalist," Courtney said to the group, as if that explained all irrational behavior. "We didn't realize you were shooting another commercial."

"Or any bank tellers," I added.

"Understandable," the director said. "Look, I can't fix your car, but I can offer you a free pass for some donuts." He dug into one of his pockets and pulled out a laminated card. "Good for a lifetime."

"Which could be prematurely shortened around here," I muttered, taking the card and looking it over. "What is this?"

"You just present it any time at a Cousins' Dozens Donuts Shop, and you get a free donut. But hang on to it—it's supposed to last a lifetime."

"My lifetime, or the lifetime of a business that hands out free merchandise?"

Courtney sighed. "Oh, please, Veronica, let's go."

I held up the card. "What does this have to do with bank robbery?" I asked. Hey. I'm a curious kid.

"Oh, we're going to make it look like a policeman is chasing a robber until he spots a Cousins' Dozens, then he stops for a donut."

Brilliant. "Well, thanks," I said with as much sincerity as I could muster. Then Courtney went off to her audition, where she lost the part because she couldn't tackle a football dummy (and thus prove that some soft drink gives even a gorgeous model the strength of a gorilla. I tell you, the people who make commercials must think we're idiots).

Meanwhile, I checked my Mazda for dents, then backed it out of the alley and waited for Courtney.

"I guess I'm all tackled out," Courtney smirked as we rounded the corner away from the interview. "Geez, you'd have to be Arnold Schwarzenegger to knock that thing down."

"Too bad they didn't look out the window and see you knocking *me* down," I said. "I think Arnold would have been gentler."

She smiled. "Did I hurt you? I'm sorry."

And then it dawned on me. "You risked your life for me," I said, pulling the car over to the curb. All at once I was too dazed to drive. "I mean, you thought he really had a gun, too, and you were willing to shield me. You put your own life at risk."

Courtney stared at me for a moment, then huge tears welled up in her eyes. Suddenly she threw her arms around me and we sat there, crying and hugging each other. She had been far more clear-headed than I was, and wanted to back out of the alley. Running toward danger was the last thing Courtney wanted to do. Yet she thought only of saving me, knocking me down if necessary, getting between me and the gunman.

"You're the best," I whispered as I held her close. "I owe you one."

She pulled back and wiped tears from her cheeks. "I hope you never have to repay me," she laughed.

And with that, we drove off for some donuts.

2

That Friday I went over to my dad's for the weekend to show him Mazda-rati's battle scars. He wasn't nearly so upset about the car as he was about my foolishness in trying to get a big story. We had a long talk; I promised to use better judgment, and we sent the Mazda in for repairs. The bad news is that I have to pay for them. The good news is that I'll get a price break since Dad is a mechanic.

Courtney thinks she should pay for half of the repairs, but there's no way I'll let her do that. She was trying to prevent a disaster; I was throwing myself headlong into one.

So the weekend didn't get off to the best start. And then, just as I was hoping to have a Friday evening to redeem myself—just Dad and me goofing around (and hopefully forgetting about my adventures in the alley)—Dad mentioned that he had a date that night. Great. Nothing is quite so weird as watching your mom or dad date.

She arrived ten minutes early. "What's your cat's name, Ronnie?" Dad's date, Gloria, used Dad's nickname for me. She had asked him out and offered to pick him up, and was now completing the role-reversal process by waiting for him to get ready.

"Mr. Emerson," I told her, quickly borrowing the name of my school principal. I couldn't tell her the truth—that I had named a tabby cat something as obvious as Tiger. She looked like the first smart date Dad had ever had, and I was afraid she'd laugh at me. The only other Gloria I had ever known was the librarian at the high school. I figured all Glorias were cerebral.

"Hi there, Mr. Emerson," she said, and scratched him under his outstretched chin. My eyes popped at the thought of someone nuzzling the real Mr. Emerson under his rigid chin. He was an impenetrable wall of disaffection for teenagers who had just survived puberty by the skin of their teeth, and, come to think of it, didn't *have* a chin. At least not one that came to mind.

Gloria looked like a stylish eastern horsewoman—tweed jacket, chestnut hair smoothed into a ponytail, laced-up leather shoes. She would probably be a date that Dad would later describe as "far out." He deliberately hangs on to that worn expression because one of the favorite Halston family reunion stories is about my asking him, at age four, how far "far out" was. Some aunt or uncle is sure to dust off this story every time we gather at Grandma Ruby's house. And everyone laughs at it, as though they've never heard it before. That, and the apple Doppler story. Once, when we had stopped for a train, I had asked Dad why the whistle went high and then low. Dad told me it was the Doppler effect. So that night, as luck would have it, we went to Grandma Ruby's for dinner. She made apple dumplings which I, at age five, called apple Dopplers, and it has become the official Halston Family Dessert. (I do not even remember this event.) This shows you how desperate the Halstons are for material, comedic or otherwise.

Soon Dad came trotting down the stairs for his date, relieving me of having to concoct further lies about my cat.

"I met Mr. Emerson," Gloria said. I cringed. "He seems very fond of Ronnie."

Now it was Dad's eyes that popped. "Really?" He was delighted to hear the first hopeful word about my relationship with the high school principal. Until now, I had been walking that fine line between Student Extraordinaire and Pain-in-the-Neck Attitude Problem Asks Too Many Questions.

I hoped Dad wouldn't ask for more details about this budding relationship I allegedly had with my principal, at least until they left. That way my cat lie could be discovered later—over dessert, perhaps. Then they could mutually discuss a way to deal with my misrepresentation of my cat's name, and whether this indicated some deep-rooted need to identify with authority, or whether I was hostile about my dad dating, since I do live with my mom most of the time, or whether I was toying with Gloria just to be cruel. Whatever they concluded, it was sure to be less condemning if they discussed it over strawberry cheesecake than if they addressed it in the heat of my embarrassment.

As they walked out the door, Dad said, "Well, see you later, Ronnie. Bye, Tiger!" Gloria beamed at hearing what she probably thought was my nickname. You could just see her light up at hearing him call me Tiger. The whole picture was probably playing in her head: Here's a bosom-buddy pal with his tomboy daughter whom he calls Tiger because they still play ball and wrestle and share inside jokes. How darling. Oh, boy. Just wait until this all comes to light over dinner.

I flicked on the TV and thought about how I absolutely must pretend to be in bed asleep when they came home. Maybe this would be their last date, and unless I stumbled into the wrong library someday, I would never have to face Gloria again. Or maybe she wasn't a librarian at all, but a manicurist like the last woman Dad dated. All I had to do was never get my nails done, and I could avoid Gloria forever. I could hear her tinny voice sniffing, "Mr. Emerson indeed!" My luck, it would get back to the real Mr. Emerson, and he'd call me into his office for a "suitable explanation."

I'm telling you, it's not easy being seventeen and watching your parents go out on dates. First, there's the basic premise: Someone is actually attracted to my mom or dad. Someone not only wants to kiss them, but in a romantic way. This, if you think about it long enough, could give you a nervous tic. Then, there's an even more bizarre possibility: Someone may even want to marry them and become a fixture in my life, despite my own feelings about this individual. This person will be spitting toothpaste into *my* sink, drinking out of *my* Taz mug, and eating undercooked eggs at *my* table. And, conceivably, two months earlier I wouldn't have known them from Adam.

Oh, I know neither Mom nor Dad would marry someone without at least getting my input. But still, the concept is bizarre: whether they know it or not, they're shopping for a step-parent for me. Maybe *I* ought to take Gloria out on the town. Have her fill out an application, interview her, get references, do this thing right. I mean, she could be *anybody!* Has she been arrested? And for what—

embezzling? Armed robbery? Does she drag around in a bathrobe until noon? Does she chew with her mouth open? Drool on her pillow? Do we know if Gloria is even her real name, or just some alias she cooked up to evade the law? Lying about a name is the first sign of big trouble. And you can quote me on that.

3

Well, you knew it had to happen. They couldn't just make conversation on their own, right? Sure enough, Dad had probed for more details about how Gloria had met Mr. Emerson, and what he'd had to say about me.

Why couldn't they have talked about world events or weather? Goodness knows you could fill a dozen dates with that, and never need to inquire about the principal of one little high school, couldn't you? Even my car wreck would have been a more interesting topic.

I had stayed in bed, faking sleep by breathing slow and steady, listening as Dad bid Gloria goodbye, then as he came down the hall toward my room, his steps familiar on the rug. My door brushed the carpet as he opened it to look in on me, then walked on to his own room.

The next morning we almost collided in the hallway, heading to the kitchen. "Why didn't you tell her Tiger's real name?" Dad asked.

Well, now I was curious as to the various theories the two of them had cooked up. I shrugged.

Dad went on. "I told her you were probably embarrassed to have named a tabby cat Tiger—like naming a spotted dog Spot. Maybe you thought she looked smart, and you were trying to impress her."

My jaw dropped and my face flamed scarlet. "That is *not* why!" I lied.

Dad ignored me and squeezed my shoulders. "You don't have to be artificial to impress someone, Ronnie. You're really neat the way you are. Besides, you were just a little kid when you named that cat—"

Now I let out an exasperated burst of air and rolled my eyes, still going for the denial. Dad just shook his head and went into the kitchen to make breakfast.

"So did you have fun?" I asked, popping two slices of bread into the toaster.

Dad tore some wannabe sausage from its package, and lined up the links in a frying pan. "Had a great time."

"What does Gloria do?" I asked, ready to cross manicures and libraries off my lifetime list.

"She's a pharmaceutical representative."

"What—she's a lobbyist?"

Dad laughed. "Ronnie, you're always thinking of the big headline story."

This is true; I am a born journalist, meant to save America, life, liberty, and the pursuit of an eventual boyfriend. "So what does she do?" I asked again.

"She visits doctors' offices to sell them various drugs—"

I gasped and whirled around. "She's a drug dealer?!? Oh, this is *just great!*"

Dad closed his eyes and smiled. "She sells *helpful* drugs, Ronnie. Come on."

"A drug dealer," I muttered, pouring the orange juice. "My dad is dating a drug dealer." Actually, I knew exactly what she did. She wore a suit and carried a briefcase full of drug samples that she would give doctors all around town, talk up the benefits of their pills versus somebody else's, maybe get a big order for antibiotics or something. Twice I had seen people like this detain my own doctor, thus leaving me to sit even longer in a drafty waiting room, and get even sicker (and thus need their medication even more; I have this all figured out).

This was very bad. This meant that I could never get sick again in my life. Otherwise, there was always a chance that I'd be sitting in a doctor's waiting room—or worse, in an examining room with nothing on but a paper smock—and Gloria would walk by and recognize me as the infamous Cat Liar. I vowed to double my intake of vitamins and stay as healthy as possible. I wrote on a mental list: *Two* apples a day . . .

"So. You and Mr. Emerson have a fun evening?" Dad grinned.

I stared at him through slits, trying to look tough. However, he had me. Unless I was going to stop referring to Gloria as a drug dealer, he was going to refer to Tiger as Mr. Emerson.

"A blast," I said, trying to block images of myself spending any kind of an evening with my principal.

"How *are* things at school, anyway?"

"Let's talk about Gloria."

Dad laughed. "Ronnie, you are so . . ." He sighed. Then he smiled as he looked up, searching for the word he wanted. I hoped a compliment was coming. "So intense, so determined. You're like a fire that wants to eat up a whole mountain."

"What size mountain are we talking?"

Dad laughed. "The biggest mountain in the world. I don't know what it is. Your ambition is so huge; you drive yourself too hard, and you don't have patience with anybody who can't keep up with you."

"Sounds like a winning combination to me," I said, my voice muffled in the refrigerator as I poked through the crispers for some cheese.

"Mr. Emerson says you come whirling into class and plow right over your teachers. You can't wait to take on the world—"

Now I turned and smiled. "And so he's decided I should skip a grade and go on to college?"

Dad just took a big breath and stared at me. "I will be absolutely fascinated to see what you become."

"I've already told you. I'm going to become a reporter and win a Pulitzer prize. I'm going to expose every corrupt politician I can. I'm going to cover bombings and peace treaty signings and elections and impeachments. I'm going to—"

Dad shook his head. "Can you do it a little less . . . vigorously?"

I leaned across my toast to look him right in the eye. "No."

He sighed. "Well, maybe that's what makes a good reporter."

I winked at him. "I'm tenacious."

"Well, would you just go a little easier on your teachers?"

"Oh, please, Dad. If I went any easier on them, they'd get replaced by a recording. I honestly think I am the only kid who ever asks one question in my English class. And this suddenly throws the world off track."

"Is that so." Dad had picked up the sports pages and was half listening to me, half reading about the World Series. "What kinds of questions are you asking?"

"Background. Before I read Edgar Allan Poe or Oscar Wilde or anybody else, I want to know their background."

Dad closed his eyes. "You know the background of those two perfectly well."

I grinned. "Yeah, but it's fun to bring it up and watch old Mrs. Cryson—"

Now Dad gave me one of his knowing glances. "See? You're a rabble-rouser."

I chomped down on my jellied toast. "Oh, all right. So I'm a rabble-rouser. Life is for living."

Dad sighed. "I'm changing my phone number. No—I'm moving to Hawaii. That way, Mr. Emerson won't call me."

"Oh, please," I said, aware that I probably use this expression way too much, but said it anyway. "You don't get half the calls Mom does. Seriously, Dad, don't you think something is the matter when they call about a student being *curious*? I mean, for crying out loud, they should be wondering if anybody has an uzi in their locker, or is selling drugs like your friend Gloria, or making death threats or something—"

Dad picked up on my Gloria comment, but ignored it. "I know you're a good kid, Ronnie. I can't think of anyone more sincere, more loyal. They know it, too. And nobody denies that you're smart, and that you'll probably set the world on fire someday. But meanwhile, you're disrupting class."

"I am disrupting a coma. Tiffany Brewster painted eyeballs on her eyelids so she'd look awake while she was sleeping."

"I don't think I want to hear about this," Dad said, aching to read about the play-offs, and not really wanting any more information about how far things have degenerated since he was in school. He raised the newspaper in front of his face.

"Okay," I said. "I'll back off in class."

"Thank you." He wasn't buying it for a second, but at least he had done his best to reform me. And, okay, maybe I could wait a few more years before exposing the truth about Paul Revere and George Washington in the school paper. You do know that Paul Revere was *not* the main hero who warned everybody, don't you? And George never had a wooden tooth in his life.

Hey. Just doing my job.

4

You have to see my mom to believe her. She is probably the most beautiful woman in the world. This, despite my flair for the dramatic, is not an exaggeration. She used to be a model, and now she runs the Mitzi Halston Modeling Studio. Her name is really Marilyn, but she has always gone by Mitzi.

I live with her most of the time, and our condo looks like the inside of a Victorian candy box. Everything is antique and swirly, covered with rose-colored satin, or tied back with ropes and tassels. She keeps the lighting soft, which casts an amber glow in the room, and makes it look as if all the fabric has been drenched in weak tea.

Sometimes I wonder if she named me Veronica because it sounded glamorous. Veronica Halston, Supermodel. Just one problem: I look like my dad. So how about Ronnie Halston, Journalist, instead?

Let me tell you, it is not only weird watching your parents date, it is weird having a gorgeous mother. The weird part is that she keeps trying to make me gorgeous, as well. (Here is a woman who likes a challenge.)

I can't remember *not* wearing makeup. Even when I was a little kid, she was dusting my cheeks with "just a little pink to brighten you up, honey." In fifth grade, she announced that I was "now a woman," and it was time to tweeze my eyebrows, and I barely had a training bra when she taught me how to outline my lips and contour my nose. While my friends were having family battles about getting their ears pierced, I was secretly hiding my earrings so the holes would grow back together.

"I just want to be a kid," I said once. It was during one of Mom's pedicure treatments.

She missed the point entirely. "Of course you can be a kid. I just want you to be a pretty one, that's all."

Sometimes I wonder if they switched babies on her at the hospital. She should have gotten my best friend, Courtney, who's a natural knockout: Tall, skinny, porcelain-skinned, thin-nosed and high-cheekboned. But then Mother would have had nothing to work on.

What do you do with a mother who waltzes everywhere she goes? Even at the supermarket, she picks up the celery with such a theatrical flourish, you'd think she was plucking a harp.

What do you do with a mother whose best advice when you tell her the kids at school are teasing you about being short is, "Rise above it, dahling"?

What do you do with a mother whose handwriting is filled with so many loops and swirls that when she writes you an absentee note, the school counselor thinks you forged it during some kind of drunken stupor?

What do you do with a mother who kisses the air by your ear instead of your actual cheek because she doesn't want to smear her lipstick?

What do you do with a mother who dyes your red hair platinum when you're in sixth grade, and then when the principal calls home to see if she knows her daughter has "gone blonde" laughs into the phone, "Dahling, don't you keep up with the trends?"

You forge your own trail, that's what you do. You resign as Guinea Pig Barbie (hey—Mom has a whole school of students to try this stuff on), and you decide to become Lois Lane and work for the Daily Planet. (Or write a book called Death by Glamour.)

My mom and dad say they split up because they grew apart. I was so young I don't really remember them together, and even today, they're so opposite that I can scarcely picture them as a couple. Dad says he married Mom because she was so high-energy, so full of life. But she became too flighty, too wrapped up in her own work. He didn't feel important to her. And Mom, who had originally loved Dad's down-to-earth style, finally saw him as coarse and unexciting.

It's funny how the things that first attract you to somebody can be the things that ultimately drive you apart.

I still love them both. I just accept the fact that Dad is a plain-spoken man, and Mom is one of those rare, bigger-than-life Auntie Mame characters who will forever sweep into a room and command attention, even if she's only taking me to McDonald's.

And, once in a while, Mom and I actually find some common ground. Just before school started, we took a horrible vacation to visit my Uncle Scott. Horrible vacations, I have decided, are often the basis for improved relationships. Something about going through a disaster together turns you into army buddies with harrowing stories to tell.

I was actually pretty excited about the trip because Mom's brother, Scott, lives in Washington, D.C. I wanted to tour all the museums, and I desperately wanted to see the White House. I mean, someday I'll be part of the Press Corps and I'll be invited to attend a presidential press conference, and it can't hurt to know my way around, right? Maybe the President would even be there! Maybe he'd look over at me, figure I'm about ten since I'm short, and say, "Hi, little girl, how are you?"

Then I'd hit him with some great zinger question about world affairs, and he'd be so surprised that he'd answer off-guard, and it might even change the course of history. To say nothing of launching my illustrious career.

Of course Uncle Scott ruined everything. Between him and his Washington socialite wife, Mia, my fate to have a boring time was sealed. Scott and Mia wanted to show Mom "the town," meaning the stores, restaurants, country clubs, parties. Somehow they even arranged it so that we not only didn't visit the Lincoln Memorial, we didn't even drive by it!

In every restaurant, Mia would ask Mom what I wanted to eat, as if I was too young to select my own food. (Meanwhile, Mia ordered drinks that, well, I don't want to say they looked like specimens of some kind, but I did double check to see if a medical lab was next door.) She even asked Mom if she'd like her to arrange for any baby-sitters.

The only time Mia asked me a direct question was when we

were driving back to the hotel on the last night. "So what do you want to be when you grow up, Veronica?"

Who asks questions like this—shopping mall Santas? "I'm going to be a reporter," I said.

"Veronica likes interviewing," Mom added.

Uncle Scott snorted. "And who have you interviewed so far?"

"Now, Scott," Mia said, patting his arm, "don't put little Veronica on the spot. After all, she's only in high school. Who do you think she could have interviewed—the governor?" They both chuckled at the impossibility of this.

Well, now I was up to my Mitzi-tweezed eyebrows with these two, so I snapped, "What makes you think I couldn't get an interview with the governor?" Mom nudged me, which I knew she would, but I ignored it.

Mia smiled as if I were stupid. "Honey, aren't you only fifteen or so?"

"I'm *seventeen*," I said with a bite in my voice.

Scott and Mia exchanged smiles.

"And," I continued, "I'll interview the governor before I turn eighteen, too. You just watch."

Mia winked at me. "Of course you will, dear." Then she began pointing out where some businessman lived who was *such* an embarrassment at the last inaugural ball.

I scowled. Mom took a deep breath and whispered, "Smile," the same way she does to her models when they forget to smile on the ramp.

Instead, I crossed my eyes.

Mia turned around and said, "Poor Veronica. I suppose Washington isn't really the most interesting city for children. But I do hope you've had fun, dear." Excuse me? Aren't the Smithsonian buildings crawling with kids?

Then Scott began snickering about some "hilarious gaff" one of the ambassadors made last week. Mia chimed in about how stimulating it was to be in the social center and circle and cycle (what— she's a washing machine?), and how pitiful it was that some politicians were in and out of office "before you can even meet their wives." On she babbled about This Famous Name and That Famous

Name, while Mother kept gushing, "Oh, Mia, you and Scott are really socialites!"

So I piped up with, "Isn't that like being a Communist?"

And instead of getting the joke, Mia laughed a condescending little titter and said, "Isn't that the cutest? No, dear, you're thinking of the word *socialist*."

"No," I said, "I'm thinking of the word *idiot*."

"Veronica!" Mom was all blinks and gulps. She couldn't even find words! It was spectacular.

Mia froze for a moment, then suppressed a snarl and said, "Excuse me?"

"Oh, that's okay," I said, leaning back into my seat. "I forgive you."

Now Mia's eyes were about to jump into the back seat with us, and Mother found voice enough to begin a flurry of apologies.

But—and here comes the good part—Mom started laughing. "Oh, I am just so terribly sorry," she lied, giggling the entire time, tears streaming down her cheeks as she fanned her eyes and tried to hold a straight face.

Fortunately, Uncle Scott was about to drop us off at our hotel anyway, and he squealed the tires as he skidded up to the curb. "Scott, you must forgive her," Mom went on, still laughing as she hobbled out of the car, trying to lean into a rolling vehicle. At last, she gave up and closed the door. Uncle Scott and his sidekick, Mia, peeled out.

"Oh, I have *got* to sit down," Mom said, still doubled over laughing, still crying like crazy. She staggered over to a planter in front of the hotel.

"Oh, Veronica," she said. "*Touché*, honey. She really had that coming."

"You're not mad at me?" I think it's safe to say I was beaming.

Mom was dabbing at her eyes now, trying to wind down. She shook her head.

"I thought you *liked* Mia," I said.

"Oh, heavens no," Mom admitted. "I was bored to tears. But Scott is family, and I tried to be polite."

"Well, I didn't mean to embarrass you," I said. "I know you've drummed—I mean you've taught manners and etiquette to me and all . . ."

We walked into the lobby, and Mom looped her arm through mine. For the first time, I felt I was floating above the carpet, in a magical place where it's okay to be pals with your mother.

"Manners *are* important," Mom said. "But so is honesty. And, given the choice this time, I think you did just fine."

We both laughed then, and Mom added, "But if you're really going to be a journalist, get ready for some heavy editing."

I shrugged. I'd worry about that after I interviewed the governor.

5

The next day we flew home, and since the fridge was all but empty, Mom and I went out for a quick dinner. While we were eating, a slender, blond man in a wool pullover sweater came over to our table. He was short, which pleased me immensely. That meant he was on my side whether he knew it or not.

"Miss Halston?"

Mother turned and smiled, extending her delicate hand at exactly the right moment. "Yes?"

"I'm Vic Jacobson, City Press." He pumped her hand hard, but she never flinched. So he works for my future employer. Someday I'll be sitting at a desk beside this guy, helping him write a late-breaking story. He smelled like cologne. I wondered if I'd be able to peg all the men's fragrances in just one whiff after I start dating. If I ever start dating.

"I'm from the advertising department, and I spoke with you last week about placing an ad for your school. . . ." Ah. So he's an ad man.

"Oh, yes! Won't you join us?" Polite again. I gotta hand it to her. I can tell she doesn't like this guy, but she is ever the gracious queen.

"No, no," Vic said. "I just wanted to tell you the ad looks terrific; it'll be out tomorrow."

Mom maintained that keyboard smile.

"I just saw you sitting here, and thought you looked like Miss Halston . . ." Then he glanced at me.

Uh-oh. Another "surely this isn't your daughter" reaction.

"Please. I'm Mitzi. With an I. And this is my daughter, Veronica."

I smiled. "With a kuh."

He laughed and I grinned. At least somebody gets my jokes. Mom didn't laugh, of course. She doesn't like me to make fun of my name (just think what she'd have to say about what I did to Tiger's).

"Well. Very nice to meet you both," Vic said, and left. I hope I marry somebody who laughs on cue like that. That felt pretty good.

I watched him walk out, then turned back to Mother. Amazingly, our little comraderie had faded and she was glaring at me. "Check, please," she said to a passing waiter. And then to me, "Don't try to be so cute with strange men. You're always putting on a big show." She was hissing through her teeth. "You think you have to charm every man who walks by, just so he'll ask me out. I don't need you to hunt for a new man for me, you know."

"I wasn't hunting for you," I said. "I was hunting for me."

Now she pursed her lips and fumed. Sometimes it's hard to tease my mom. This was one of those times.

That night, just before I went to bed, I knocked on Mom's bedroom door. "Can I come in?"

"Of course, darling." Mother was sitting up in bed reading a beauty book, with pink satin sheets pulled over her legs. A Kodak moment.

Incidentally, she has a bed that is not to be believed. I tried to lie down on it once and was nearly thrown into the next county. I swear, it must have garage door springs for mattress springs. What will we do when someday she replaces it, and we haul it (cautiously) onto the front lawn for a garage sale? Some unsuspecting customer will lie down on it, get catapulted into our silver maple tree, and sue us for a million dollars.

On the other hand, I can't picture my mother running a garage sale. But I can't see her in the circus, either, which is where that bed belongs. They could roll it out underneath the trapeze artists, and if one of them fell, the bed could fire him back into the air, high enough to grab the trapeze and go on with the show.

I wonder if Dad ever slept—or tried to sleep—on this bed. I'd say that's grounds for *something*, right there.

How does Mother sleep on it? Has she discovered some trick to running and jumping so as to land smack in the middle where the springs aren't so tight? Or does she just sneak up to it and slide carefully onto its surface, like a burglar snaking along to avoid radar beams? NASA should look into this bed.

Anyway, I apologized for the smart comment I'd made over dinner. "Well," she said, "you're a smart kid, so I guess that figures." Then she looked at me and smiled. "I'm really proud of you, you know."

What? Veronica Halston's mother is proud of her plain, vertically challenged kid? I always feel I can't measure up next to the models she raves about. This was music to my ears.

"I'm excited about your interview with the governor, too. When are you going to call him?"

Mom believed in me! Banner headlines:

SHORT, RED-HAIRED STUDENT DEAD FROM SHOCK.
Corpse was smiling.

"Really?" I croaked. "You're excited?"

"Of course! I thought it was a wonderful idea—even if it was Mia's. So when are you going to call him?"

"I don't know," I shrugged. "I'm scared."

Now Mother was surprised. Me—the outspoken kid who was still jumping off the roof with an umbrella five years after all the other kids had stopped—admitting I was scared.

Mom laughed. "Well, you've heard the pep talk a million times. You know what to do."

True; Mom was always waving the "You Can Do It" banner; it was part of her beginning charm course. I resolved to call him the very next day, and kissed her good night.

I walked a few steps toward the door, then turned around again. "Mom?"

She looked up.

"What if he says no?" I asked.

"Argue."

We both grinned. "I knew that," I said. And with that, I tossed my red curls and strutted off to bed.

*   *   *

The next day I thought I'd have some big, dramatic answer when Mother burst through the door in late afternoon, wondering if I was the next "Woodland and Bernstein." (It's Woodward, but this was not the time to correct one's supportive mother). All I could tell her was that the secretary had taken my name and would get back to me.

"Give her three days, then you call her."

"Mom, I can do this myself."

"I know. I'm just so excited to tell everyone you're going to interview him."

Suddenly something in all this sweetness tasted bitter. My chest felt constricted for a second as I understood the real reason why Mom wanted me to interview the governor. She must have seen my face fall, because she quickly said, "Honey, it's just that I want the whole world to know what a great reporter you'll be!"

"Mom, if I'm a great reporter, the whole world *will* know." I took a deep breath and hid the prickly hurt behind teasing. "Besides," I said, "I'll probably have to wait forever for that kind of thing. Until I'm at least . . ." Here I groped for an unfathomable ancientness. "Thirty!"

She smirked, fully aware that I deliberately seek out opportunities to needle her about aging. "You'll make it," she said. "Despite your twisted sense of humor. I really think you have what it takes."

I wonder how many journalists in town have stage mothers cheering them on as they write obituaries and cover political speeches. Oh, well, who can knock it?

"Courtney wants me to come over to study tonight. Can I go?"

"Sounds fine. She's doing the big show for me. Did she tell you?"

Yes, of course she told me. She told the entire school. In fact, if she gets any better at spreading news, I'll be out of a job. Courtney's my best buddy and I love her, but I worry about her. She's really taking this skinny model stuff seriously.

"She's got a great look," Mom went on. "We're doing a Native American thing, and she'll be perfect for it." Mom unfurled her cape with her usual flourish and hung it in the closet. She was coordinating and emceeing a fashion show for a big luncheon next month. The biggest designer in town was letting her use some of his gowns, and Mother was on an absolute high over it. "Can't you just see Courtney in black sequins? With that silky black hair?"

Courtney has jet-black hair and giant, Bambi eyes. If she does indeed become an actress, I'm sure her agent will be selling her as everything from an Eskimo to an Italian. She has perfect cheekbones and full lips. Basically, we are talking Pocahontas.

"And that tiny waist! She'll look like an Indian princess!"

Mother floated into the kitchen and took a salad bowl out of the refrigerator. Little beads of water were clinging to the underside of the plastic wrap, ready to rain down onto the lettuce below. Mom has a way of delicately pinching the plastic with her fingers so she doesn't scrape her nail polish. Dad and I just dig our nails under and rip the plastic off.

Courtney had graduated from Mother's Professional Course, and had invited half the high school to this fashion show. "I think she's awfully skinny," I said.

"Skinny, but not awful," Mom said. "She has a long, graceful look." Mom began tossing the salad with mounting enthusiasm as she envisioned her show. A few pieces of lettuce landed on the counter. "She's perfect."

"Yeah, well, Courtney doesn't think so," I said. "She thinks she's fat. Fat, can you believe it?"

"Oh, all models think that. They're always dieting, trying to take off a pound or two." Mom reached for the plates.

"Not Courtney. She wants to lose *ten* more pounds."

"Well, that's not really necessary."

"Not necessary? It's ridiculous." I stole a piece of romaine and popped it into my mouth. One thing my mother really makes well is a good salad dressing.

"When you see her tonight, remind her to be on time for the first rehearsal, will you?"

"Sure." But Courtney wouldn't need reminding. Mom practically pummels her students with all the rules of professionalism. If one of the girls is late, she'd better be dragging her own severed leg as an excuse. "Don't be late, don't whine, don't forget to tape the bottom of your shoes. Bring two extra pairs of pantyhose *without toes*, and an extra slip. Don't wear jangly, distracting jewelry. Bring a strapless bra. Bring a black bra. Know your clothes ahead of time and bring the right shoes. Cover your head with a scarf when you pull clothes over your head, so you won't get lipstick on them. Don't smoke or eat in the dressing room. Bring hair spray. Check the lineup and be ready way ahead of time. Keep your curling iron hot. Tuck in the price tags, or save them to pin on later. Hang the clothes up again. Help each other. Practice your turns. Wet your lips. *Smile.*" I often help my mom backstage, and I have heard these rules a zillion times.

Sometimes, when I'm at my dad's garage, I'll hand him tools. Over the years, I've learned about all the tools from cam shaft breakdowns to timing valves, and all the parts between a piston and a universal joint. It's really a bizarre contrast to have an inside track in such opposite worlds: I actually think I could throw together a fashion show and rebuild an engine in the same afternoon.

And I am banking on this paying off someday, once boys discover me. Finally—here will be a girl who can help them change the oil AND keep lipstick off her clothes at the same time. What a catch, eh?

6

Music was blaring so loudly from Courtney's house that you could hear it six doors away. Since my car was still in the shop, I rode my bike over and parked it by their garbage cans. Courtney was inside, exercising in striped leotards.

"You look like an elongated bee," I said.

She laughed. "Like 'em? They're new. I've just got to do five more minutes' worth. Sit down."

I sat down and watched her exercise. My own theory is that it's not good to sweat. Sweat is your body's warning system, telling you to stop what you're doing immediately. Someday I am going to expose this whole sweat concept in a front-page article, full of studies that show the multiple health problems of big sweaters. Not sweaters that you wear, you understand. Sweaters as in "perspirers." On second thought, since there's no real word for people who sweat a lot, this could get kind of confusing. People might think I'm accusing an item of apparel of being a health hazard. Some joker would write a letter to the editor, suggesting that I was attacking fashion to rebel against my mother. Okay, scratch the perspiration piece.

But I'll still stick to reading for exercise. That way I'll have strong eyeballs.

"Mom says you're going to look great in black sequins."

Courtney stopped in mid-split, her eyes and mouth stretching open with delight. "All right! She got the gowns!"

"Yeah. She said to tell you to be on time to the rehearsal."

Courtney sat with her legs open in a V and bounced her head to one knee. "Are you kidding? I'll be there early just to try on those gowns!"

I was happy for her. She really loves this modeling stuff, and after watching her on the ramp, I have to admit she's good. But I worry about her weight. She's so thin; I swear, she looks anorexic.

"You really look skinny, Courtney," I said.

Courtney looked up and smiled. "I wish!"

"But you are," I said. "Look at you. Your collarbone looks like a ballet barre."

"Twenty-six, twenty-seven . . ." Courtney ignored me, counting her repetitions.

Sometimes I wonder if I'm the only person in Courtney's life who is worried about her health. Courtney's parents are fantastic—fun to be around, and obviously in love. But they don't seem concerned about how thin she is. In fact, they always seem to be trying one fad diet after another themselves, always talking about being fat and needing to lose weight. Ironically, neither of them is even heavy.

And to think Courtney wants to lose another ten pounds. I mean, this gorgeous girl actually looks in a mirror and groans. If I looked in a mirror and a face like Courtney Calhoun's was looking back at me, I'd pass out from sheer joy.

Sometimes Courtney will eat like, well, like me. We'll go out for pizza and she'll have three or four slices. But then she'll go to the bathroom and throw it all up. You couldn't pay me to throw up. But Courtney's gotten to where she can't help it; it's like her stomach has turned into a trampoline. What's she going to do if a guy asks her on a date to a picnic? Where will she lose her lunch—behind a tree?

One time I sat down and talked to her about it. "You are the neatest girl," I said. "Why don't you believe that and like yourself the way you are?"

She smiled and squeezed my hand. "Veronica, my church teaches that same thing. In fact, because we're daughters of God, we often talk about being of royal birth—princesses!"

I grinned. Of all the people I knew, that description fit Courtney best. "So how come you don't believe it?" I asked.

"Oh, I do. I love my church, Veronica. I believe in God with all my heart. I know he sent Jesus to die for us, and I know he restored

Christ's original church to the earth. Someday I want to tell you about that. We call it a testimony, and I do have one. I just—I don't know. I don't feel good enough or something."

"Wait a second," I said. "What do you mean about Christ's original church?" That sounded intriguing.

But Courtney looked down and blinked away sudden tears. "I just . . . I'm so ashamed of this stupid eating problem," she whispered. "I'm not a good example of what a Mormon girl should be. I—I really want to tell you about my church, but . . ." And again, she looked as if she was ashamed.

I remember wishing I could climb into her brain and shake out the knots—get rid of this obsession with thinness. She didn't seem to be doing it for attention, though she will always be one of those women who draws attention. It was as if she was trying to measure up to somebody's crazy standard.

"Courtney," I said, taking her by the shoulders, "you are so much better than you realize. I'll bet you're everything your church teaches. You're the best friend in the world."

She hugged me then, but there was still an uncertainty in her eyes.

I've gone to Courtney's church a few times. Never for Sunday services, but to their youth nights, which were pretty fun. Mom and Dad have never actually taken me to any particular church, but I can remember sitting on Grandma Ruby's lap and hearing her wobbly voice tell me about the birth of the baby Jesus, and it's still one of my favorite Christmas memories.

I often wonder about religion, God, and what life is all about. It's not something I share with all my friends, but I have a few theories of my own (probably this does not surprise you). First of all, I think entrance into heaven ought to be based on more than just saying you believe in Christ. I think you ought to *live* what he taught. I mean, he said to be like him, right? And he was always *doing*, not just talking. He helped people, loved people, really put it all into action. I can't understand religions that teach deathbed repentance—that you can be a horrible person right up until the last minute, then suddenly say you're sorry. I'll tell you, if *I* were guarding the pearly gates, I'd say, "Not so fast, buster," to those folks.

Another of my ideas is that if we go to heaven when we die, we must have been in heaven before we were born. It seems logical to me that our spirits lived before birth. One big circle, you know? Besides, people are so complex—even little kids—that it's hard to imagine their personalities just springing into being at birth. Also, if you don't start out with a personality at birth, how do you explain the different dispositions of newborns? I mean, even in a litter of puppies, you find that some are frisky and some are not. I figure we came into this life with pretty definite personalities already.

I also think you should keep learning after you die. I mean, much as I hate certain classes and homework, I like discovering new stuff and feeling the rush of excitement when I master something. To die and spend the rest of eternity without learning a single new thing sounds so boring I can't even imagine it. It would be like getting trapped in an elevator with Aunt Mia forever. I figure we'll be learning in some totally new way—maybe not even in classrooms, but tapping into the brain waves of geniuses or something. Cool.

Courtney was still exercising when I finally turned off her music and insisted that she study with me. I really like her family. Except for continually bouncing from grapefruit to popcorn diets, they're normal. Her parents are always joking around, and her two little brothers idolize her. Even though the boys fight with each other, they always treat Courtney like a princess. I offered to buy them once, and they got a big kick out of that. Ever since then, her brothers have liked me, too.

*   *   *

In the car pool the next morning, Courtney looked really ashen and weak. "You okay?" I asked, taking her arm.

"Yeah. But I'm *starving*. I didn't eat breakfast," she whispered back.

I took an apple out of my lunch (one of the two I am still eating every day in order to avoid doctors' offices and thus Gloria) and shoved it into Courtney's hand. "You are turning yourself into a baby bird," I whispered. "You keep this up and I'm feeding you worms, I swear it."

Courtney grinned and buried her chin in her coat. Courtney has always been my bud. I rescue her, she rescues me. One time some kids were standing on the tables in the cafeteria, making fun of me. They were pretending the tables were my mom's modeling ramps and here came her daughter, clomp, clomp, clomp. One kid put a hand on his hip and strutted around like a stripper. Mr. Mannavey, the history teacher (who knows about teasing—the kids call him Manna Ray), came and grabbed the kid, but not before Courtney threw a well-placed blob of spaghetti sauce on the jerk's shirt.

Another time, knowing I loved the book *The Little Prince*, Courtney hunted all over town for a special edition she knew I wanted. In exchange, I bought a movie cell for her from her favorite Disney movie, "The Fox and the Hound."

I guess that's kind of like my friendship with Courtney, in fact. We aren't the look-alike friends you see malling around (you know the type—two girls who cruise the mall, wearing the exact same hairstyle, makeup, clothes, shoes). Courtney and I look as different as salt and pepper, but we *like* that.

I also like the fact that Courtney isn't boy-crazy. I watch other girls at school gasping and giggling about their latest crushes (usually in the restrooms at the mirror, where they slather on makeup, enjoying a taste of forbidden fruit, since their parents don't want them to wear any, and where I am usually rubbing mine *off*), and I think how glad I am that Courtney isn't all gaga over some guy. We talk about so many other things *besides* just guys. Of course, we talk about them, too, but not with the shrieks and dramatics of some of the other girls. Mostly we share our crushes in whispers and grins, and would *die* if anyone else knew how we really felt.

Courtney, being a real knockout, has not escaped the attention of the guys at school. But they kind of hang back, probably because she's like my mom—almost so pretty that she's intimidating.

Lots of guys are my friends, and they act more relaxed around me than they do around the girls they have crushes on. I think I have this figured out: it's sort of like I'm in the safe zone, and they can be themselves around me. (It doesn't hurt, either, that my mom has a modeling studio. Who knows? I may come in handy someday as a connection for them.)

Not that I wouldn't love to be gorgeous. But as long as I'm not, I'm looking at its up side. And there's a big one: I am getting a fantastic peek into the mind of the mysterious male. They're letting their guard down around me, and I'm discovering that cocky guys are actually insecure, class clowns are often covering up something sad, and smart guys—even if they're shy—usually have the sharpest wit.

Not only do I feel like a reporter getting an exclusive interview, but I'm learning stuff about guys that is going to come in handy once I "blossom," as Mom keeps insisting I will. Hey, blossom or not, I'm going to know so much about men that I'll be way ahead of the game when I finally date. Even now, I see girls in complete confusion about what a guy means when he teases them, and I almost feel like offering my services as a translator, because I know *exactly* why he's acting that way. It's a cool feeling, like knowing a secret language.

Anyway, since I'm destined to be a writer, I can't let boys distract me from my goal. If I get all wrapped up in a boyfriend, I may miss a good story. Okay, I don't really believe that last part; I was just seeing if you were awake. Actually, I'd love it if I could move past the kid-sister phase and turn heads like Mom and Courtney do. But as long as I don't, I can always say I'm holding back on purpose to focus on my career!

Once in awhile a really smart kid, like Eddie Dregman, will hint that he'd like to get to know me away from school sometime. But that's about the limit to my romantic powers.

Right now I'm in like with Jimmy Murdock. He's in my English class and is the most totally fine guy you have ever seen. If there's one thing I have, it's exquisite taste. Unfortunately, Jimmy also has terrific taste and goes with Amy LaRoyce, the best-looking, most popular, most feminine creature ever to walk the halls of Jefferson High. (Courtney's just as pretty, but not so flirtatious.) So I dream—along with the rest of the female studentbody.

Well, you can imagine the collective heartbeats that skipped when we got to school one morning and heard that Jimmy and Amy had just broken up. For awhile, it looked as though they'd win Cutest Couple at the end of the year; but it seems that Amy is going steady with the basketball team all of a sudden.

Lauren Bochley, who always knows the latest rumors about

everything and will no doubt be the gossip columnist at my newspaper someday, was telling about it in the bathroom, where we all congregate before going to class. This is a female ritual, one hard to imagine being duplicated in the boys' bathroom. I'm only guessing, of course, but it stretches the imagination to picture guys hovering around a mirror, giggling and combing their hair, talking about girls and trying on new eye shadows. Somehow the image just doesn't fit. We girls, however, wouldn't miss it.

"What a stud—how could she dump him?"

"Oh, they'll get back together."

"No way. Every guy in this school is after her now."

"How would it be!"

"And every girl is after Jimmy."

They all had something to say about it as they rummaged through their purses for combs and lipsticks.

"Veronica, you sit by him in English. Why don't you ask him about it?"

I laughed and pretended to be a TV news reporter, using Lauren's brush as a microphone. "And so, Mr. Murdock, tell us exactly what happened. Did she slam the door on your foot, or spit in your face, or exactly what?"

The girls all started laughing.

"Tell us the emotions you're feeling now, Mr. Murdock. America waits to hear your reaction. Are you angry? Crushed? Happy?"

Now all the girls were pretending to be Jimmy, talking into the brush at once, all trying to come up with funny lines. I finally rolled my eyes and laughed along with them. "I'm sure I'm going to ask him about it in English," I said sarcastically.

Now the giggling died down. "Why not?" Lauren said. "I mean, he talks to you all the time. You can get him to open up."

Good old Veronica, sister to every guy at school. "I just can't," I said. "It's too personal." I was going to say that I'd never repeat anything he said, anyway. Didn't they see that they were asking me to betray a trust? What if Jimmy was really heartbroken? Some friend I'd be, rushing back to the lavatory mirror to report my findings. No way.

"Maybe he'll just start telling you about it," Brooke Cooper said. Brooke thinks that every guy in school is dying to pour his heart out to me. She thinks I have some magical way with men that makes them confide secrets. Okay, I do have something. What I have is a mother who runs a modeling studio, and every guy at school knows it.

"Maybe Cryson will ask him to write an essay on it, then give an oral report," I said. "Or better yet, an assembly."

"Okay, okay," Lauren snapped. "So don't ask him. Leave us all in suspense." Lauren always resorts to using guilt when she can't bull-doze you. I can picture her entire marriage.

"Gimme a break," I laughed. "I don't even know anything about it! And I don't *care* why the Jimmy and Amy Show has been canceled. I never watched it anyway."

That was a lie, of course. Like I said, every girl at school was utterly infatuated with Jimmy Murdock. I used to drool right along with the rest of them as he and Amy would walk together. It was like watching the Royal Couple stroll by.

What would be fun to watch now would be the abounding rumors about the breakup. And, naturally, Amy would be sweeping the entire high school's male population off its feet. I wondered who Jimmy would choose next. How could he top Amy?

I really liked Jimmy and hoped he wasn't too heartbroken. I mean, I liked him as well as you can like somebody you've hardly spoken to. I wasn't exactly in his crowd, so we'd never actually had a conversation.

Then, in English class, a strange thing happened. You are not going to believe this, but I looked up from my paper and Jimmy Murdock was staring at my legs. If you knew my legs, you'd know this was the height of hilarity. I laughed.

"Jimmy, mind if I ask what you're doing?"

He didn't blush, but he did grin and look busted. "I was just . . . uh . . ." Then he got that cocky expression on his face that is on a lot of guys' faces these days, and said, "Guess I'm a leg man."

The bell rang, and it took me a minute to realize this was the actual bell, not some crazed noise in my own brain. Somehow I got to my feet, and I could feel Jimmy staring at me as I walked—

red-faced and with my heart pounding—from class.

This must be how pretty girls feel all the time, I thought. And Jimmy Murdock had just given me my first feeling of prettiness. *I would marry you tomorrow, Jimmy Murdock.* Any guy who can stare at my short, chubby legs—without laughing—has my heart forever.

For the first time ever, I counted every minute through the weekend, until it was Monday and I could go back to school. Then all morning I was in a fog, watching the clock and waiting for English class to roll around. Could it be that Jimmy Murdock *did* see something in me? Was he perhaps a wise, mature, sensitive man trapped inside the body of a hunk? Could it be that he cared about my inner qualities, my tender soul, my real personality? Had he broken free of the ridiculous emphasis on physical beauty that seemed to possess every other guy at school? Was he ready for a real woman?

Miss Korsky, the home economics teacher, interrupted my daydream. "Veronica, are you all right?"

Sewing machines were humming all around as everybody tried to put zippers into their A-line skirts ("the most flattering style for every figure," Mother would say).

"Huh?" Thank heavens she snapped me back to reality before I needed a straitjacket. *Get hold of yourself, Veronica. Jimmy Murdock would not consider you his type. Not by a mile-long modeling ramp.* "Oh, I'm fine. Sorry. Just thinking."

Miss Korsky smiled. She likes me. (She knows I can put together a fashion show, that's why. First, she'll have us sew these ghastly, lumpy skirts that none of us will ever wear again. Then she'll say, "Veronica, I know you've helped your mother put on lots of fashion shows. Would you like to be in charge of ours?" And, of course, I'll have to do it; otherwise I'll never get an A in this class, because I sew like I walk.)

At last it was time to go to English class. As I walked down the hall, I could feel butterflies in my stomach. My fingers left damp spots on my notebook. Ugh. Mother would say to dust them with baby powder or an unscented anti-perspirant. Like I'm going to pop by my locker for a palm treatment.

Jimmy was standing in the doorway and smiled as I walked in. Then he followed me to my desk.

"Weren't you waiting for somebody?" I asked him, nodding toward the door.

He grinned. "Yep. You."

I gulped about a gallon of air and wondered if it would be cool to burst out laughing. I decided it wasn't an ace move.

"You really look nice today," he said.

I just swallowed. *I'm dreaming, right?*

Jimmy went on. "How's your essay coming?"

I could feel myself blushing, and the more I worried about it, the hotter my cheeks felt. "It's finished." My voice was a squeak. I could have died.

"Think you could help me with mine? I mean, you're good at English. Maybe you could help me."

"Sure." *Are you kidding? I'd write you an entire book.*

"Well, I want to do mine on hunting," Jimmy said. "You know, deer hunting."

"Which side are you taking?" Cryson had asked us all to write an opinion essay, picking an issue and defending one side.

Jimmy laughed. "Pro, of course!"

Of course. I smiled. But inside I cringed. I *hate* hunting. Until now, I've even hated all hunters. And now Jimmy Murdock wants me to help him promote it. "What do you want me to do?"

"Well, I'm really not sure how to get started," he said. "Could you maybe write down some ideas—you know, give me an example of how I should do it?"

"Okay. I'll bring it tomorrow."

He beamed. "Cool. You're really great, Veronica." He was giving me that hungry stare again.

"Well, uh, thanks," I stammered. "You're all right, too."

He sat down beside me at his desk. "You know what else I like about you?" he said.

My legs? Be serious.

He was. It wasn't my legs. "You never look down your nose at anybody," he said. "Amy did all the time."

"Well, people with noses as big as mine don't get to look down them very often," I said. Oh, DUMB! Headline: VERONICA IS A NITWIT. Why did I have to say that? What a stupid thing to say. Mother would have had a fit.

"And you're funny," he said. "I like your sense of humor."

But not the nose. Notice he didn't disagree with me about the nose? Oh, well.

That night I wrote the best essay of my life. In favor of hunting. Thank heavens my name wouldn't be on it. These things can surface later in life, you know. I don't need some pro-murder paper coming back to haunt me.

In English class the next day, Jimmy took the paper and grinned again. I can't believe how white his teeth are. And his hair is so thick and soft-looking. I wondered what it would be like to touch his hair.

"Wow," he said, scanning it. "This is great! Thanks!"

"It's not a final draft," I lied. "It's just to give you an idea."

Jimmy looked over at me and stared at my legs again, even though I was wearing pants this time. "You give me a *lot* of ideas," he said.

Now my hands were so wet I couldn't hold onto my pen, and it slid from my fingers and rolled a couple of inches across the desk.

At lunch, Lauren came and sat down by Courtney and me in the cafeteria. "So?"

"So what?" I didn't want to talk about Jimmy, but I knew that's the information she was after.

"So did he say anything?" Lauren was smacking a wad of gum.

"Yeah, he did." Now Lauren and suddenly the whole gang seemed to gather around, all listening with wide eyes.

"Gimme a break, you guys," I said. "I'm not E.F. Hutton."

Courtney laughed and winked at me. She winks when she likes the jokes, and just laughs along with the others anyway when she doesn't.

They kept staring and waiting. I stared back.

"Come on!" Lauren couldn't stand it.

"He said he's writing his essay on deer hunting."

Now everybody groaned. Somebody in back said she'd like to be his dear, and they all laughed and scattered to different tables to eat.

Courtney shook her head. "We ought to make up something really hilarious and tell them. String them along."

"How about this one," I said. "Let's tell them that Jimmy is actually in love with someone else. That he stares at her legs every day and waits for her by the door and asks her to help him with his homework and says she gives him *ideas*. And her name is Veronica Halston."

Courtney didn't laugh. She smiled. "Hey, you're not making that up. I know you, and you're serious."

I chuckled and looked away, wishing my neck weren't crimson.

Now Courtney's mouth was open in delighted surprise. "It's you, isn't it?" she whispered. "Man, that is fantastic! Way to go, Veronica! Can I tell? This is so awesome."

Now I wished my mouth weren't the size of Virginia. "No, please," I whispered back. "Don't say anything. I mean, I'm really jumping to conclusions, I think."

"No you're not. Jimmy *likes* you. He must, if he's doing all that. Wow!"

I kind of groaned and started giggling (if you're in high school and you don't know what else to do, 85 percent of all coeds choose giggling). "I'd die if it got back to him," I said. "I swear, I would lie down on Cryson's desk and die right there in English. Then she'd ask everybody to describe the event in 100 words, and I'd die *again*."

Courtney laughed in genuine happiness for me. "I won't tell. But I'm excited. You have *got* to give me every detail!"

I sighed. Even though I regretted having such a big mouth, at least now I had somebody to talk to about it. Maybe this is why newspapers were founded, because it's impossible to contain a gigantic news story in one short body. Me and Jimmy Murdock. Unbelievable.

8

I was a zombie through all the rest of my classes. In algebra, Ms. Francesci asked me to write on the blackboard, but my hands were so sweaty they completely soaked the chalk and then it made big, lumpy lines on the board that you couldn't erase. I mean, have you ever tried to write with a piece of wet chalk? The stuff turns to mortar, I swear it.

There I was, smack in the front row, watching the teacher try to erase my work and it could not be budged. Worse, it was *wrong*. Mistakes emblazoned in history. Lumpy scribbles forever etched into time. And there was Ms. Francesci, working up a sweat of her own as she tried to get them off the blackboard. She kept snapping her head around and glaring at me as if I had deliberately perspired on her precious chalk and caused a class disruption. I slid down into my seat, my face a deeper crimson with every passing second.

The only benefit of it all was that she was forced to abandon her former plan, which was to cover the board with equations—probably much harder ones—and instead decided to show us a corny film about a little stick figure and his metric ruler. I immediately recognized this movie as the throwaway filler it was, and took the opportunity to fully fantasize about Jimmy.

Here's what I imagined. Jimmy drives his car over to my house—it's shiny and fast (the car, not the house) and rings the bell (on the house, not the car). He's nervous, but in such a haze of love he doesn't care.

I answer the door wearing the world's most flattering jeans and a $300 sweater that I miraculously found that morning in a gutter (fantasies have to move along; you can't slow down to include reality). Also miraculously, I have shed twenty pounds and I look ravishing and svelte.

Mom is in the kitchen baking cookies and wearing bifocals.

Jimmy walks in after giving me a giant hug—the kind sailors give their sweethearts as they leave for the war in old movies—and he goes into the kitchen for a cookie.

Mom drops her rolling pin on her foot and it breaks (the rolling pin, not the foot). Jimmy and I help my poor, klutzy mother to a chair, and when we go under the table to pick up pieces of the rolling pin, Jimmy kisses me. It's incredible. Having never been kissed, except by spitty-mouthed little boys in the second grade, I can only tell you that it was wonderful.

We crawl out from under the table and Mother claps her hands together—make that unmanicured, chappy hands—and says, "Jimmy! You are so thoughtful and sweet! Veronica has told me so much about you, and I can see that you're every bit as charming as she's said."

Jimmy gives me a squeeze and I smile shyly. Then I say, "Mom, don't you think Jimmy should do some modeling?"

Jimmy looks stunned. He's so humble, he can't believe I'd suggest it. "You really think I could?" he says.

My daydream zooms forward to Mom's studio. Photographers are clustered around Jimmy, completely ignoring the other models. A man steps forward and hands Jimmy a studio contract from MGM. Would he do a screen test?

Jimmy looks at me in surprised delight, but partly for my opinion and approval, too. I nod and Jimmy signs in a rugged, handsome signature with black ink.

For moral support—and because he can't stand to be away from me for five minutes—Jimmy asks me to go along with him. I hesitate, but he begs and pleads, so I consent.

In Hollywood we're given the royal treatment, and directors wearing felt berets give us tours of the studios. Signs that this is just a make-believe shooting are posted in alleys all over town. Suddenly a producer dashes up and cries, "We've lost the leading lady! You—Veronica—can you act?"

And then, as the very proof he needs, I lie and say, "Can I act? Can fish swim? Can birds fly? I was the lead in all my school's musicals! I've been making commercials since I was a baby! I've been *this close* to Broadway," I hold up a pinch of air, "but I lost all the parts because I'm so young."

The director rocks back on his heels in astonishment. "No!"

"Yes!" Jimmy and I say in unison.

And he signs me up to be Jimmy's leading lady. In our first scene, we're galloping through a beautiful meadow. I'm a beautiful Indian maiden, and Jimmy is a cowboy who I find unconscious in the Grand Canyon. I nurse him back to health, and now we're riding to my village, totally in love.

Suddenly we come to a raging river. Jimmy's horse stops abruptly, throwing Jimmy into the icy torrent, where he's heading for a waterfall and disaster. Still weak from his scorpion bite—yeah, I like that—he can hardly swim a stroke.

But I, the perfectly toned and athletic Indian Maiden who happens to teach Squaw Aerobics, dive gracefully into the water and swim to Jimmy's rescue. My tan skin (okay, waterproof makeup) is gleaming in the water, and my rawhide dress clings to my perfect curves. Hey, this is getting good. Jimmy sees my hand reaching for him, and grabs it just as the music reaches a crescendo. I pull him to shore and he lies there, exhausted. His shirt is torn, revealing his muscular chest, and I gently touch one of his scratches, which then magically heals. Indians know how to do these sorts of things.

Amazingly, Jimmy has sudden strength and sits up. "Princess"—lemme see, need a name here—"Running Fawn," he says, "you saved my life!" Then he takes me in his arms and pulls me close against him. He turns my face toward his, our lips are about to touch—

"VERONICA!" Ms. Francesci's voice pierced through my fantasy like a whip, and I nearly fell out of my chair.

"Veronica, I've been calling your name for five minutes. Where are you?"

She meant, "where are you mentally?" and if I told her she'd never believe it. Nor would she believe the company I was keeping.

"I'm sorry," I mumbled. Some of the other kids were giggling, but I was actually less embarrassed than I was mad at being brought back to reality. If I'd been dreaming in my sleep, and if Ms. Francesci had been an alarm clock, she'd probably be smashed against a wall right now. Instead of chewing me out, she ought to be grateful that this was not the case.

"Veronica, I asked what you thought of the film," she said, her voice tight with irritation.

Film? Huh? I was still partly shooting a film of my own. "Oh, it was a *fab*ulous movie, just incredible," I said.

The whole class burst into hysterical laughter, and she dismissed us. I can't figure those students out; they actually thought I was kidding.

9

That afternoon I took the bus over to Mom's studio to ask her if I could study at Courtney's house again (and no doubt talk about Jimmy Murdock). Mom was in pink leotards, leading an exercise class.

"Never do sit-ups with straight legs, ladies. Always bend the knees." Mom liked to call her students ladies, and always spoke in a clear, well-modulated voice. She didn't even strain to speak as she did the sit-ups along with her panting students.

"And we always touch our toes from the sitting position," she went on, bending gracefully over her now-straightened knees and lightly brushing her toes with her glossy pink fingernails. "NASA scientists say you can stretch your back too far if you touch your toes from a standing position." (Who would have thought that NASA scientists would be quoted in a modeling studio?) The girls all watched her and tried to copy her limber movements, their faces scrunched with effort.

Mom's studio always reminds me of cotton candy. Everything is pale mauve, soft and billowy. Except for the crisp lines of the gigantic mirrors (which seem to cover almost every wall), you feel almost as if you're floating on a pink cloud.

The reception room has a giant bulletin board plastered with photos of her models, and from there a wide hallway leads to several classrooms. One of the rooms contains a ramp where the girls practice their runway techniques and turns. Another has a long mirror surrounded by makeup lights, where the girls transform themselves with the wonders of blush and mascara. Still other rooms are for lectures, exercise, TV commercial classes, and etiquette.

Since Mom was busy, I wandered on to the next classroom. Alicia, one of Mom's instructors, was explaining to a dozen girls which hairstyles best flatter each face shape. Everybody wants to fake an oval for some reason, but I'm not sure what makes oval so hot.

"Okay, Jenny, your face is square," Alicia was telling one of the students. "That means your forehead, cheeks, and jaw are about the same width. You've shaded the jawline, which is super and really softens the edge, but you need to part your hair in the middle and let a few bangs fall over the corners."

Why not just tell the unfortunate girl she's a blockhead? Poor Jenny must feel like an absolute cube.

Alicia went on. "Madison, your face is the diamond. You want to create the illusion of width where your face narrows, like right here on your forehead. Bangs are good. And to make your narrow jaw look fuller, you can bring a little hair into this area of your cheeks."

Better yet, Madison, grow a beard. Then nobody will know you have a (horrors!) diamond-shaped face. Actually, with her widow's peak, she might be considered a heart shape. If she can marry a guy with a club and a spade, maybe they'll have a full deck. It's incredible. People actually pay thousands of dollars for this. Just as I was turning to leave, Alicia said, "Oh, hi, Veronica. This is Miss Halston's daughter, everybody!"

Oh, please. Don't say that. Another room full of astonished faces.

"Veronica, come up here and show the girls how you do *your* hair."

Ha. Not a chance, Alicia. I waved my refusal. "I'm just waiting for my mom," I said. "Besides, since I couldn't come close to the oval shape, I'm having cranial surgery."

A couple of the girls laughed. Two of them near the front of the room raised their eyebrows, obviously intrigued and excited to think such a thing exists, and might just save them from certain doom.

I wandered back to Mom's exercise class to wait, settling into a puffy pink sofa in the back of the room. I thought about my plan to study at Courtney's, and wondered if we'd end up talking about boys the whole time instead. Who knows—maybe we'd talk about Tony Rulini, this guy who's already in college and on whom Courtney has a crush the size of Italy. I'm all for him because he's smart. Courtney's all for him because he has huge, melt-down brown eyes and muscular shoulders. I guess those are good reasons, too.

But her mom goes into a frenzy if Courtney even mentions his name. Mrs. Calhoun is scared of Italians because Courtney's aunt married one, and then the guy ran off with another woman. I hope motherhood doesn't bring everyone that kind of crazy logic, but my mom evidently uses it, too.

Here's an example of Mitzi's Famous Logic: "Nobody ever credits their long life to knuckle-cracking." This profound statement is supposed to discourage her students from taking up this "revolting habit," as Mom calls it.

Another sweep through the powers of sound reasoning is this one: "If you wear nubby pantyhose, that's the day you'll get in a car wreck." Supposedly the wearing of pantyhose that have begun to pill—in front of emergency room technicians—is not only the worst embarrassment one can incur, but can actually *cause* traffic accidents.

Anyway, Courtney's mom is convinced that misery and unhappiness will be Courtney's automatic return if she invests in an Italian. "Well, you know what they say," I told her once, "Fettucini breeds contempt."

Brittany Gladman stopped exercising during the leg raises and came huffing to the back of the room. Brittany's mom makes her take these classes to get her weight down. She's one of the few girls who is realistic enough to see that she will never become a model. Of course, when you're over 200 pounds and only five feet tall, your options become clearer.

I tried to make friends with Brittany at first, thinking we had something in common—not that I'm heavy, though I'm clearly no model type. But Brittany was so whiny and self-centered that I soon lost interest.

"My doctor says to stop when I get tired," she panted. "I have shingles all around my ribs. When I sweat, they get worse."

Good grief. She doesn't need a doctor; she needs a roofer.

"That'll be all today," Mother said, switching off the aerobics tape. "See you next time, darlings."

Brittany got up and padded over to Mother. "I had to stop,

Miss Halston. My doctor says—"

"That's all right, Brittany," Mother said. "I understand."

Well, I don't. What's this poor girl supposed to do—never work the weight off because she's not supposed to sweat? Some choice: die of obesity or shingles. And I think *I* have troubles.

The girls filed out, and Mother smoothed her hair in an elegant gesture. Mom, who sweats Chanel Number Five, then draped a burgundy towel around her neck. How does she do everything with such flair? I tried to swing a towel around myself that way when I got out of the shower once, and nearly knocked myself out.

"Hi," I said. "Need any help with the show?"

"No, no, everything's coming along fine. But thanks for asking, darling. And anyway, I have a date."

"Oh. Well, great." She goes out occasionally. So far I haven't thought much of her suitors; a row of Ken dolls might be as intelligent. But I don't say much. "Mind if I study at Courtney's, then?"

"*Veron*ica, I should say not! I want you to meet him."

Uh-oh. Could she be serious about this guy? I could see she was immovable about letting me go to Courtney's house, so I didn't press it. Besides, I had probably told Courtney too much, anyway.

I sighed as I got into Mom's car, wondering what this date of hers would be like. To be honest, Mom does not have a great track record in picking men. Somehow they seem her opposite—anything but elegant and aristocratic. But, to her credit, she has never come close to marrying any of them.

One guy was arrested for rolling back speedometers in his Lincoln-Mercury lot (Mom has not had terrific luck with automotive types). I spotted him as a wheeler dealer the minute he walked through the door and began snapping his fingers and slapping one fist into his other hand. I could just picture him saying to some wimpy customer, "Only half a grand down, and you can have this little baby—just like that!" *Snap, pop, pop*! He wore big, gloppy gold rings—no doubt from some shady shenanigans—and a hideous sports jacket that my mom later admitted "probably got him convicted."

She'd be a great judge. "White patent leather shoes in November? Thirty days hard labor. Orange lipstick with pink blush?

That'll get you five years without parole. Chewing gum in public? Life sentence." She'd be a tough one, all right.

Another time, Mom went out with a guy who was so boring that I thought about switching my future from journalism to medicine, and selling recordings of this guy as cures for insomnia. He hung around one time talking about drill bits and plywood. Honest. He'd been building a shed or something, and he sounded like a slow-motion recording of the assembly instructions. Mother hung on his every word—an act I found worthy of an Academy Award. Best Actress in the motion picture *Bored with Boards*, for her portrayal of a captivated captive audience. Leading man was Boris Moore (get it?), noted for his still-life characters. Supporting actress, Veronica Halston, gave a memorable performance as the zombie daughter whose occasional sighs and blinks provided comic relief in this otherwise tragic saga.

After he left I said, "If that man were ice cream, he'd be vanilla ice milk." And to think I lost a week of TV privileges for that remark.

A few years ago I did like one of her dates, however. His name was Jarvis, and he was a spelunker—an explorer of caves. His job probably fell under the forest ranger category; he simply scouted the state parks for new caves, then went in to see if they were safe or interesting for tourists (they were usually neither). But this is a job *made* to be embellished, and that's where Jarvis and I—both natural exaggerators—found a world of common ground.

"Isn't it dangerous?" I egged him on, my mind racing with images of vampire bats, sudden deep holes, and witches' cauldrons.

His eyes flashed. "Sure, but *somebody's* got to be the first person to take the risk." And, in most cases, somebody probably was, leaving beer cans and rags for Jarvis to kick through. Still, I liked to think of him as an adventurer in the Christopher Columbus vein, probing new frontiers and feasting his eyes upon glimmering coral stalactites, embedded emeralds and glittering gold. Who knows—maybe ancient thieves (now reclining as skeletons amid poisonous vipers) had stored bars of gold or treasure maps in these caves.

Perhaps a similar dream kept Jarvis going into dark crevices and crags that never seemed to reveal anything but dead animal bones, dusty gray rocks, and an occasional spider. I used to brag to my fifth grade friends about Mother's professional spelunker, telling wildly exaggerated—okay, completely fabricated—tales of his bravery and daring. He was worth at least three term reports. Thus, when she stopped dating him, I was disappointed at having to end my glorious lies. Since then, the dates have drifted by in bland contrast to my explorer.

I wondered what Dr. Palucci would say about my mother on his radio show. Sometimes I listen to talk radio when the music compartment in my brain is full. It's like eating—music is the main course. But sometimes, even when you can't take another bite of chicken, your dessert compartment is empty and you can eat a whole cheesecake. That's how it is with me and music. Sometimes I want some variety, so I listen to the local talk station.

Dr. Palucci is the station's resident psychologist. I've thought about calling him, but it's pretty hard to stay anonymous when you have to tell the listening audience that your mother runs a big modeling school in town and you're the ugly duckling daughter who has every indication of remaining a duck. I mean, that pretty well narrows it down to the Halstons, you know?

Besides, they'd probably sandwich my call between a man who wants to be a ling cod and a woman who can't get her boyfriend to make a commitment (so what else is new?). Then Dr. Palucci would probably advise me to a join a club of people who share my same interests. He always falls back on that when he gets stumped. Or maybe he'd tell me that looks don't matter and I shouldn't worry about it. The problem is that I've been raised in a world of cold cream and cotton balls. Beauty is what puts a roof over my head and clothes on my chubby little body. Without glamour and vanity, where would my mother be? And then where would that put me?

Maybe he'd tell me to sit down and have a nice chat with her. Tell her I feel inadequate and disappointing. But I know what would happen if I tried this: Mom would launch into one of her positive thinking/you-can-do-it lectures and tell me I can be anything I want to be.

What if I wanted to be Chinese? Or five-foot-eight? What if I wanted to be a sweepstakes winner? Or a stagecoach driver? I mean, there are some things wishing won't bring. What if I wanted to be Jimmy Murdock's girlfriend?

Mom introduced her dark, handsome date as Antonio. "So you're Veronica," he said, trying to conceal his amazement.

"Welcome to the anticlimax department."

Mom threw me an icy stare, and I knew I had committed Charm School Crime Number Four: Don't insult yourself.

But actually, I was just trying to let the guy know he could drop the "I'm so enchanted to meet you" act. Sometimes I just don't say the right thing. This was one of those times.

Then Mother corrected me publicly, which, if ever I teach a manners class to a bunch of girls who look as though they stumbled head-first into puberty, I'm going to add to the list of Charm School Crimes. Never humiliate your kid in front of others.

"Veronica, you shouldn't put yourself down like that," she said. "It pressures others into giving you compliments."

I just smiled and went back to my geography textbook. I had four chapters to catch up on for a test. Mr. Elkin, one of my teachers, had announced that he would be "quizzing" us tomorrow on our reading. Swell. An Elkin "quiz" is like a legal bar exam. If he says he'll be giving a "test," you may as well prepare to meet your Maker and go through the final judgment itself.

"Veronica, Antonio is a psychologist," Mother said, nodding proudly at her date. "Isn't that interesting?"

What's more interesting is that he's an Italian. I wondered what Courtney's mother would say. "They're starting a psychology club at school," I said.

"Oh, are you going to be in the club?" Antonio asked.

"No."

"Not interested in human behavior, eh?"

Who is this clown? How can he make assumptions like that? I hoped I wouldn't get a bill for this conversation.

"I'm not interested in the kids who are signing up," I said.

"Really? Why is that?"

I looked up from my reading, where I had re-read the last sentence four times due to all these interruptions. "They seem like a bunch of mixed-up kids trying to find themselves, and they spend a lot of time sitting around and 'opening up.'"

Antonio frowned. He reminded me of a Dr. Seuss character, so I looked down at his feet to see if his toes were curly, but they were stuffed into wing tips, so I couldn't tell.

Just then Mother gasped, "Oh, look—one of those awful brown things!"

We followed her frantic stare to the ceiling by the draperies, where a bitty little spider was clinging for dear life, probably wondering who the hysterical woman beneath him was.

"It's just a spider," I said, getting up from my chair. "I'll get a paper towel."

"No, I'll do it," Antonio said, sounding not at all comfortable as Rescuer.

I ripped a paper towel and a half off the rack. They never tear in straight lines; have you noticed that? When I went back into the living room, The Brave Antonio was standing on a chair—*my* chair—in his wing tips and swatting at the ceiling with a newspaper. Here is a guy, I thought to myself, who does not kill many spiders. Any fool can tell you they only fall down and run away when you do that.

Fortunately for the spider, Antonio was not very tall and never really got a good swat at him, only a light brush stroke, which knocked the spider effortlessly off the ceiling and gently down to the carpet below.

"Watch out!" It was a high-pitched shriek like one my mother might use, but two things were wrong. One, my mother never screams (it's a Charm School Crime). And two, it emanated from the quivering throat of our dear Italiano. He had reached out and clutched at the draperies and was more or less hanging by them, supporting only part of his weight on the chair, which itself was beginning to teeter. Mother helped him down and I dived for the spider, which was scurrying away to friendlier territory.

Mother smoothed Antonio's jacket. She now had shifted, with marvelous aplomb, from the Damsel in Distress to Florence Nightingale. "Are you all right?" she asked him.

Embarrassed, as he should be, Antonio said, "Of course. After all, it was only a little spider."

Darned right. So why did you scream, eh? Not interested in spider behavior, eh? I excused myself to my room, and within a few minutes the gallant knight had hopped onto his trusty steed (in this case, a Lexus), and whisked Mother away to dinner.

When she came home, she tapped on my door. "Well, what did you think of him?" she asked, beaming and glowing as if she'd never seen a spider in her life.

"I think he's a big boob."

Mother frowned. "You're grounded for a week."

"A week?" I was so stunned I nearly fell off my bed. "How can you say that?"

"One week, young lady. And if you continue to make rude remarks about Dr. Palucci, I'll make it two."

"Two?!" My jaw dropped. "Wait—Dr. who?"

"My date," Mother said. "No more back talk about him."

"Wait—Did you say Dr. Palucci?"

"That's right."

"The guy on the radio?"

"Yes. So?"

Now I slumped back onto my pillow and groaned. I couldn't believe that spineless wimp was the same all-knowing doctor who people tuned in to every day, trusting him to help them sort out their lives. And to think *I* had almost called him for advice! What irony. What rotten luck. What—hey! What a great source of material for Cryson's next assignment: An essay on fallen heroes.

The next day at school, Courtney and some of the girls said they wanted to go look around the mall that night, and they wanted me to come along.

"I can't. I'm grounded."

"Why?" Katie Cosgrove, whose parents are so lenient that she didn't even get grounded when she ran away in a sailboat—a stolen sailboat, yet—always finds it amazing that Courtney and I get grounded periodically.

"Believe me," I said, "you'd never believe me."

"Why—what did you do?" That was Courtney.

"I said her date was a big boob."

Everybody stared at me for a minute, then two of the girls busted up laughing and everyone else joined in. Even I did.

"Be serious," Katie said.

Now I *really* laughed. "I am. And he was." But I decided not to reveal his identity.

Courtney laughed and wiped her eyes. "Your mom is the only person I know who is stricter than *my* folks."

The bell rang and we all split for classes—they for the easy subjects of gym and music appreciation, and I for the torture and agony of Elkindom.

Mr. Elkin, besides giving the toughest, meanest tests in the known world (about the *un*known world), also has the most distracting habit of any teacher I've ever had. He keeps licking his lips and biting off little pieces of skin. Yet the man does not bleed. He must be a Martian. I think you can get skin cancer from doing that, but I'm not sure.

I wish some of my teachers could take Mom's poise course so they could weed out all their bizarre mannerisms. And so that Ms. Francesci, one of the math teachers, would learn not to wear horizontal stripes. Watching her is like watching a TV that has lost its vertical hold. You walk out of that class with glazed eyes and a permanent fear of giant bumblebees.

Elkin passed out his tests, and *I* wished I could have passed out. They'd rush me to the school nurse (who Courtney thinks is the local dope peddler), and I'd get to go home and not take this horrible exam. Until tomorrow.

I waded through 200 questions about unknown rivers, mountains, longitudes and latitudes before I finally resorted to Plan B, which is my last-ditch effort to complete the test before the bell rings, and which consists of answering B to all the multiple choice questions I have skipped so far.

At long last the bell rang, and I did my Charlie Chaplin impersonation as I walked up to put my test on Elkin's desk. All I needed was a cane. The way I figure it, if I'm going to bomb on a test, I might as well do it with style.

I saw Jimmy on the way to English class, and he said he wouldn't be there today. He had to have his picture taken for the yearbook with the rest of the football team. Then after English there was a school assembly. Nearly everyone had found their seats by the time I got to the auditorium, so I slipped in on the back row and sat a few seats away from some tenth graders.

The lights dimmed, and the studentbody president came out to tell everybody about the terrific entertainment to follow—something about an accordion player, a dramatic reading, and a film. Suddenly Jimmy Murdock slipped into the seat beside me. "Hi!" His teeth sparkled in the dim light.

"Hi," I said, my throat suddenly dry.

"You waiting for anybody?"

I shook my head. I had tried to find Courtney, but missed her. My whole body was tingling.

Then Jimmy winked and put his elbow on the armrest so that his arm was touching mine. I thought I would die. *What if he takes my hand? What if my hand is clammy? What if someone sees? What if my heart jumps out of my chest?*

Finally I regained enough sense to turn my face toward the stage, but I had no idea what was happening there. My full attention was focused to my left, on Jimmy and what he might do next.

Turns out he did nothing but sit there. Still, that was enough to send me reeling. Every once in awhile he'd lean toward me and whisper something and I'd laugh—although in retrospect his remarks weren't all that funny. But here I was, sitting in the dark with Jimmy Murdock. I was in heaven.

"Well, gotta run," he said just before the assembly ended. "I gotta take care of some football stuff." Then he darted out of the auditorium, leaving me weak and flushed as the lights went on. I stood up, still in a daze, and walked slowly to my next class. Just think—he left football to come and sit by me, even though he had to come late and leave early.

"Veronica!" Courtney was beside me, shouting my name, just as I got to the door. "I've been calling you for a mile." Then she lowered her voice. "I feel like I'm going to pass out again." Courtney'd been dizzy lately, and now she bent over to put her head between her knees.

"You okay? You need to eat something."

"I'm okay." She sighed and stood up again. "Just another headache. So what's up?"

I grinned. "Courtney, you'll never believe this. Guess who came and sat by me in the assembly?"

Her mouth fell open as I told her what little there was to tell.

"Wow—I'm glad I got stuck backstage," she said. Then I remembered that she had signed up to help some of the school officers with this latest "show." She squeezed my arm. "This is so cool."

I smiled. "Don't tell."

* * *

When I got home from school, I called Governor Barrett's secretary. She said she still couldn't give me an answer yet, and asked me to call again Monday.

I wished that I had an older sister or somebody, so I could ask her, "Am I being put off or what? Does she really want me to call again, or is she politely telling me to get lost?" Then I decided that I had youth on my side, and if I called again and she asked me why I couldn't take a hint, I'd be able to blame it on inexperience. How did I know the way you're supposed to deal with a governor? On the other hand, his secretary was probably too busy to play games; she must really have wanted me to call again.

* * *

And then Lauren Bochley and two other girls from our crowd called to say they'd heard about my sitting with Jimmy in the assembly, and they wanted to know all about it. I closed my eyes. I tell you, nothing gets by those tenth graders.

"We're just friends," I said, then quickly explained that I had to go, and hung up.

The next day I was prepared for the whole school to be buzzing with the new rumor. Probably the only thing that kept it from sweeping the studentbody was the sheer unbelievability of it. No doubt every kid who heard that Jimmy Murdock was now interested in Veronica Halston was passing it off as a joke.

So I made it to English with a minimum of attention. At least until Jimmy walked in. He kept looking over at me and smiling. Finally class ended, and he walked out with me. "So when are you going to invite me over?" he asked.

It caught me off guard. "Oh—anytime," I said.

"How about tonight?"

"Uh, okay. Sure." My brain had left for the Bahamas; what did it matter?

Jimmy winked and disappeared.

And then I remembered: I was still grounded. What was I going to do? I knew I couldn't call Mom and ask her to give me a night's reprieve—not at a school phone with kids walking by and eavesdropping. So as soon as I got home, I dialed the studio.

"Mom, you've *got* to let me have a friend over tonight. I already said yes, and I forgot about being grounded—"

"That's no reason."

"I know, but Mom—it's the cutest guy in the entire school, maybe in the whole world. He sort of invited himself over, and I couldn't get out of it—"

"Veronica, you are grounded."

"Oh, please, Mom. I'll do anything—anything! I'll be grounded for another whole week if I can just get through tonight."

"Who is this young man?"

"Jimmy Murdock. I think he likes me. And he won't stay late, I promise. But I *can't* call him and tell him not to come over. I would die. Honest, Mom, I would *die.*"

"Jimmy Murdock—isn't he the one who plays football?"

"How did you know that?"

"I've heard some of the girls here, talking about him."

Megan Pitney and her gang, no doubt. They chase all the jocks. "Please, Mom."

She laughed. "Oh, all right. This once."

"Thanks!" I said. "I owe you one. I owe you twenty."

"I won't forget." I could tell she was smiling. Or maybe it was relief that some guy finally noticed her daughter. Yikes—I suddenly hoped she wouldn't rush home to do a makeover on me.

Fortunately, she had to work late, and still wasn't home when Jimmy arrived at approximately 7:22 and 43 seconds. I gave him a SevenUp and he sat on the sofa and drank it. We talked, mostly about Cryson's class, and in a few minutes, Mom drove up.

Jimmy made a great impression. He seemed to perk up and put on as much charm as Mom does sometimes. They talked about modeling, and Mother asked him about football. I could tell she really liked him. What a relief; I wanted things to go smoothly and I, usually the one with plenty to say about everything, was finding myself almost tongue-tied.

"Maybe I'll drop by your studio and see about the male modeling classes," Jimmy said. "Sounds kinda fun."

"Oh, do," Mother said. "You'd just love it. And you'd be so good at it, I can tell."

"You got a deal," Jimmy said, and rose to leave. "See you at school, Veronica." Then he jogged out to his car and drove away.

I sat there, smiling.

"Well, I can certainly see why all the girls like him," Mother said.

"Yeah," I sighed. But I couldn't help wondering: what did Jimmy see in me? Was Mother wondering the same thing? Oh, well. Maybe it was just a case of opposites attracting. I didn't care; I was just glad it was happening.

I took Jimmy's glass and SevenUp bottle back into the kitchen. Just think: Jimmy Murdock drank from this very glass. Too bad I couldn't mount it in a scrapbook.

12

Dad picked me up the next morning before school and took me to breakfast. We're both early risers, and once a month or so we hit the all-you-can-eat pancake joint. But this time my mind was on Jimmy Murdock, not Belgian waffles. Twice Dad asked if I felt all right. I was completely zoned out, daydreaming of Jimmy. Was this how it felt to be in love? Was this how Dad felt about Gloria? Was it how Mom felt about Dr. Palucci, heaven forbid? Hey—I needed to figure out a way to get Dr. Palucci together with Gloria. That way, Gloria could slip quietly out of my life and I would never again have to worry about calling Tiger Mr. Emerson. Dad had been out with her again, by the way. I tried not to cringe visibly when he said this.

"Dad," I asked as he twirled the syrup carousel, looking for maple, "what's it like to be in love?"

"Oh, no you don't," Dad said, wagging a finger at me and getting a panicky look in his eye. "You just forget about boys until you're . . . I don't know . . . sixty-five or something."

"Oh," I said. "Good plan."

Now he was rolling his eyes and moaning. "My little girl," he whispered. "Please say it isn't so."

"Oh, come *on*," I laughed, seeing at once where my tendency to exaggerate came from. "I just asked what it felt like."

Now Dad was holding his head in his hands. "But you're *thinking* about this sort of thing. This is the beginning of the end." Now he had syrup on his forehead, and when he dabbed at it with a napkin, pieces of white paper stuck to his skin.

"The end of what?" I stared at this hysterical man. Why don't I ever have a video camera in my hands when I need one?

Dad dunked his napkin into his water and began splashing his forehead. "First the tooth fairy, now this . . ."

"Good grief, Dad. It's not like I've eloped with some guy—"

Dad froze in mid-splash, his eyes like shiny Christmas balls. "Don't even say the *word* elope. Don't even *think* about it. You have at least twenty more years before you even need to *date*. Why, when I was your age . . ."

I could see the man needed to recline on a Barcalounger with an ice pack, so my chances of getting a serious answer were basically zip.

Finally it was time for school, and I watched the clock all the way through first period. On the way to my second class I happened past the computer lab, and saw Jimmy talking with his friend, Brad Derisch. They were sitting behind a couple of screens, and Jimmy's head was turned so he couldn't see me. I stood in the doorway for a minute, but he didn't look up.

And then my heart stopped. I heard Jimmy say, "Hey, it's the old Murdock Charm, what can I say?" Then he and Brad laughed and Jimmy said, "She'd probably do *all* my homework if I asked her to. She wrote me a whole essay on deer hunting. Probably stayed up all night!" Then they laughed again.

I started going numb, and I couldn't move. It felt as if I was suddenly encased in ice.

"When she introduces you to Megan, have her pick somebody for me, too," Brad said.

"You got it. I'm asking her about it today."

"Good deal."

"That is," Jimmy went on, "if I can stand it. When I sat by her in the assembly, let me tell you, man . . ." Then Jimmy barked.

Brad laughed. "Force yourself. She's got the connections we need."

"That's what I keep telling myself . . ."

Suddenly my feet were moving, and I was running for the bathroom. When I burst in, Lauren and a new girl were at the mirror. I ran right by them and slammed the door to one of the stalls.

"Veronica, are you okay? You look white as a sheet," Lauren said.

I leaned against the door and closed my eyes. The one time I want to be alone, and I get Lauren and some new girl standing right behind me, trying to talk.

Just then somebody else walked in. "Veronica's sick or something," Lauren announced, directing attention to my stall.

Somehow I managed to find a piece of my voice. "I'm okay," I said. "I'll be fine." I felt nauseated but I didn't want to throw up. My face was cold and clammy and I felt weak. Maybe I'd pass out and die, and then an ambulance would come and take me away. *Then Jimmy would be sorry*, I thought. And then, *no he wouldn't. A creep like that would never even associate my death with his cruelty.*

I had never hurt so much. How could he do this to me? I started to cry, silent tears rolling down my face. I pulled off a strip of toilet paper to dab at my eyes. I felt utterly humiliated. All this time I was being played for a fool—and who knew how many guys were laughing at me behind my back? He was using me to get to Megan Pitney; I should have known. She's the equivalent to Amy, but at Wescott High. Another cheerleader. How could I have been so naive as to think Jimmy really liked me? How could I have been so gullible as to write that stupid deer-hunting essay for him? I imagined the whole school knew about his little joke.

And Courtney. Bless her heart, she didn't laugh at the idea. She honestly thought it could have happened. I wished she were here to cry with me, to be furious with Jimmy.

I can't stay at this school, I thought. *I'll have to transfer. I can't face these kids anymore.*

Suddenly, Courtney was tapping on the door. Lauren had grabbed her in the hall and told her I was throwing up in the bathroom. "Veronica, should I go and get the nurse?"

"No. I think I'll just go home," I said, trying not to sound as if I'd been crying. The bathroom was full of people, and this was no time to explain things to Courtney.

"You sure?" she asked.

"Positive. Thanks, anyway." I was determined not to let people see I'd been crying. The whole school would know how crushed I was. I wanted to get out of there. No way could I face Jimmy in English. I wondered what sly trick he had devised to get me to introduce him to Megan.

I never felt so stupid in my whole life. I thought about how close he sat to me in the assembly. All that whispering—just to fatten me up for the kill. No wonder he slipped in late and left early; he didn't want anyone to see him sitting by me! And all that friendly chatter with my mom—all to get an invitation to come and prowl around the studio. I burst into silent tears again.

Finally, I caught my breath and dried my eyes. Another wave of girls came in, and I hid in my stall until they were gone and classes had started. When I was sure I was alone, I went out to the mirror and looked at my red eyes. At last Mitzi's Makeup Tricks would come in handy. I dropped some Visine into my eyes and smeared concealer stick over the red patches around my nose. I took a deep breath.

Anger was welling up inside me now, and I was tempted to go to English and devise some way to get even—maybe send Jimmy on a wild goose chase that would serve him right. Offer to do an essay for him and misspell everything. But I decided I was too heartbroken and would never make it through class without sobbing. At least it was Friday; maybe I could recover over the weekend. Also, I was going to my dad's tonight, and maybe he'd have some good advice about dealing with guys.

I stuck a note in Courtney's locker to let her know I went home and I'd call her later. Then I called Mom to come and get me.

"Veronica, what happened?" she asked when I got into the car.

I started crying again, just like a little kid whose skinned knee doesn't hurt until he sees his mother. I told her the whole story. "We have to move," I wailed. "I can't face him ever again. I can't face all the kids; they're all going to know about it."

"Oh, Veronica, you're making too much out of this," she said. "Okay, Jimmy is an immature little boy. But just say to yourself, 'Who needs him?' and move on."

My shoulders shook as I breathed in chattered jerks. She didn't understand. She could drop guys and "move on" with such ease, like all pretty girls. Where one guy falls away, another moves into place.

"I can't," I said. "I'm too embarrassed."

"You'll feel better tomorrow." Mom just didn't get it.

"But he's so rotten," I said. "He tricked me!"

"Maybe you assumed too much. Did he ever actually tell you he saw you as a girlfriend?"

"Mom, guys don't do that. They don't stop you in the hall and say, 'Oh, by the way, we're a couple now.'"

"Well, there are plenty of others out there."

But that wasn't the point. It wasn't that I wanted all these imaginary others. I felt cheated and deceived and humiliated. "I hate him," I cried.

"Get hold of yourself, Veronica. You're being boisterous."

Being boisterous might very well rank as the Top Crime of all Crimes in my mother's teaching manual. To be labeled boisterous is to be somehow less than human—a member of some primitive, loud, and disgusting species. The opposite of feminine is not masculine; it's boisterous. As a child, if ever I was playing and squealing with my friends, Mother would stick her head into my room and say, "Not so boisterous, darling." I would gasp and wilt beneath such a shocking accusation, and would immediately modulate my voice into a more ladylike register.

Her parting advice for any occasion, be it a slumber party or an excursion to the zoo, was "Don't be boisterous, Veronica." In third grade, I became so infuriated with Emily Dockstrom, a little brat if ever there was one, that I started shaking and turning purple and finally blurted out, "You're *boisterous!*"—at which point I trembled in fear of having called her the worst name imaginable. As recompense for this savagery, I kissed up to that fool Emily Dockstrom for the whole rest of the year.

"I don't care if I *am* boisterous," I said to Mother. "Jimmy *used* me! I hate him!"

Mother shook her head. "You need a hot bath."

My mother's solution for every problem is a beauty bath and facial. "There's nothing a good pedicure can't take care of," she once said in a modeling class. "That's why they call them pedi*cures.*"

Mom made me put on a cucumber mask and get into the bathtub. I stared at my reflection in the wide metal faucet and was even more depressed. Against the green clay of the mask, my eyes looked even redder. My hair was tucked into an orange shower cap that mother calls her "turban," and I looked, for all the world, like a space alien.

Mom dumped some bath crystals into the water. "Here. Swish these around."

"Mother, my entire life is over and I want to die. I don't feel like swishing."

"Don't talk; you'll crack the mask."

Oh, please. Somebody have mercy and shoot me. I've just had my heart chewed up and spit out by the love of my life, and my mother is worried about cracking the mask.

When I finally got out of the tub, my face felt like the inside of your mouth when you eat a lemon. "I have lock-cheek," I said.

Mom was there with her chilled astringent and cotton balls, dabbing my cheeks and forehead. "Did you do your cuticles?"

I looked at the little stick-on clock that hangs on the bathroom mirror. *Three more hours until Dad rescues me.*

Mom sat me at her makeup bar and stuck pieces of cotton between my toes so the fresh polish wouldn't smudge. "How about Merry Berry?" she said, reading the label on the bottle of nail enamel.

Help me, anybody.

She shook the nail polish like a maraca as the little BB inside clicked against the bottle's edges.

The world is coming to a screeching halt, I'll never be able to face another living human and I'm having my toenails painted Merry Berry red. Headline:

PROMISING JOURNALISM STUDENT
GROOMED TO DEATH
*Friends tell of recent tragedy
that makes it a blessing*

Veronica Halston, 17, daughter of the Famous Mitzi Halston and the Not-At-All-Famous Harold Halston, died at 2:46 p.m. during another of her mother's "forced beauty treatments."

Doctors are blaming nail polish asphyxiation and skin suffocation due to applications of deadly cucumber masks and cancer-causing nail polish with intelligence-insulting names.

Friends and teachers say the loss is a big one for American journalism and society in general, but sources close to the victim say it was for the best.

"She was just jilted by her boyfriend," said Courtney Calhoun, the victim's best friend. "Everyone hates him for it, and I'm sure it will come back to him," she added.

When pressed for a comment, Murdock, the suspected cad, said, "How could I have been so stupid? She was the greatest thing that could ever happen to me, and now she's gone! It's all my fault!"

Murdock confessed to posing as a decent human being in order to use the victim to get to another woman. He also admitted fraud in persuading Miss Halston to write a deer-hunting essay which is now under consideration for the Pulitzer prize. . . .

"I want you to lie on my slant board for twenty minutes now," Mom said. "That will give your toenails a chance to dry and get the circulation going under the skin on your face. Your skin is your largest organ, you know. We have to take good care of it."

I groaned and walked silently to her slant board.

"Gravity is the natural enemy to smooth skin," she says in her classes. "Lying with your feet elevated will not only reduce wrinkles, it will slim the ankles."

Once I was situated on the padded board, she left me alone and I resumed crying. The tears ran into the hair around my temples, and I knew my hairline would friz. Mother would want to put setting gel on it to straighten the hairs back out again. Then a moisturizing treatment on my face, peaches and cream blusher, frost moss eye shadow with pearl foam highlights and apricot blaze lipstick. The perfect recipe for a broken heart.

13

Finally Dad pulled into the driveway, and I ran on my Merry Berry toes to the window and waved.

"See? I told you everything would be better after your bath," Mother said. "Tomorrow you won't even know who that boy is."

She opened the front door with a sweeping gesture and said, "Well, here she is!" as if she was unveiling a masterpiece.

Dad stepped into the room and looked over at me. "What happened?"

"What do you mean, 'what happened?'" Mom snapped. "She looks gorgeous!"

"Yeah, that's my point," Dad said, helping me put on my coat. "Whenever she looks gorgeous, something horrible has happened."

I smiled. As heartbroken as I was, it still felt warm and wonderful to know that somebody was really in tune with me.

"See you Sunday," I said and kissed Mom's cheek.

"Be good. Eat right." Mom leaned over as I walked out the door and whispered, "and don't *worry*."

Dad buckled his seat belt and we drove off. "So?"

And then I lost it again. Mom's makeup dripped onto my collar the whole way to his house as I sobbed through the story.

When we got to Dad's place, he held me. "That stupid jerk," he said. "I'd like to call up the slimy moron and tell him just what he's done."

"Oh, no—I'd die," I said, pulling away.

"I know. I know. But if his dad ever brings in a car—"

I laughed through my tears. "Give him the works!"

Dad smiled, then winced. "This must really hurt," he whispered.

"I can't face my friends," I whined. "They'll all know."

"Okay, Ronnie, look. First of all, almost nobody knows, and the ones who do will see Jimmy for the jerk he is. How would you feel toward him if he'd done this to Courtney?"

I thought about it. Dad was right. Jimmy was making himself look rotten. "But I want to get back at him," I said. "I don't want him to get away with this."

Dad sighed. "Getting even always hands the lion's share of the power over to the other side."

I didn't understand. "Huh?"

"When you take the trouble to get even, you're forced to admit that the other side really hurt you. Right?"

"I guess so."

"So you're handing them another victory—all the power again. Don't go for revenge, Ronnie. He isn't worth it."

"But I'm so *mad* . . ."

"And you have every right to be. But don't let Jimmy turn you into somebody like he is."

I sighed. "Good point."

Dad smoothed my curls. "You're a princess. He's a scuz."

I laughed. Me, a princess. Just like they said in Courtney's church.

Now Dad grew stern. "I mean it, Ronnie. You *are* a princess. You're special. You're smart. You don't need some guy who can't appreciate all you have to offer. If he's so stupid that he can't see how wonderful you are . . . who needs him?"

I smiled and wiped my tears on my wrist.

Dad went on. "Ronnie, here's how you ought to feel. Can I tell you how to feel—is that okay?"

I nodded.

"You should feel sorry for that poor, lame idiot. He probably won't grow up until he's forty-five years old and twice divorced. Think about how much more mature you are than he is. Have you ever really talked to him?"

I swallowed. Come to think of it, Jimmy was gorgeous and

charming, but not terribly witty or clever. He didn't strike me as brilliant, or even as someone who's driven enough to go places in life. He seemed like a gorgeous guy who was coasting along on his looks.

"How did you know he wasn't all that smart?" I asked.

Dad smiled. "Guys like him blanket the earth," he said. "You'll meet lots of them, and the story is always the same. So just feel sorry for him. That's all he deserves—pity. You've learned a lesson here, Ronnie. And if you can learn from every setback, you'll never be the loser."

"Oh, Dad, you make it sound so easy."

"Do I? Well, I know it isn't easy," he said. And then suddenly, "It's like religion, Ronnie. Truth and good morals aren't always easy. But they're the right way to live."

I sat up. "Religion?"

Dad chuckled. "I know you haven't heard me say much along those lines, but lately I've been thinking more about it. What's that saying—'If the straight and narrow path were used by more people, it wouldn't be so narrow'?"

I smiled, intrigued. "So . . . you're like, going to church and stuff?"

"Oh, I've gone a couple of times with Gloria."

Ach! Gloria again! I glanced over at Tiger, who was curled up, asleep in a slant of sunlight, oblivious to the trouble he'd caused.

"Well, I guess they teach honesty and stuff," I muttered. "Like about cats' names."

Dad grinned. "They talked about that just last week! A whole sermon on how important it is to tell the truth about the name of your cat. Then your name came up, Ronnie."

"Very funny. Oh, my sides."

"Actually," Dad said, "they talked about forgiveness. I think Gloria has not only forgiven you, but forgotten all about it. Now you need to forgive yourself."

I shrugged. "Well, I'm not forgiving Jimmy Murdock."

Dad rumpled my hair. "You will one day. Any guy who doesn't like you needs his wheels aligned."

I smiled. "And maybe his axle broken."

"Aw, don't you worry about that. He'll be bringing himself

plenty of misery without you helping him. Guys like that always do."

I smiled. "Thanks, Dad."

"It's the honest truth," he said. "You're a Maserati, Punkin'. Jimmy's just an old Rambler."

That night I slept like a brand new car, all tucked away beneath its cover in the quiet stillness of a peaceful, moonlit night.

*   *   *

Saturday morning the weather was bad, so we stayed inside playing games, reading, and cooking. Dad makes great cinnamon rolls, and we both gorged until we were sick. "Best stomachache I've ever had," Dad groaned from under a newspaper on the sofa. He had the paper folded over his face and it gave him a funny, faraway sound.

I laughed. "I thought you were asleep."

"Can't sleep. Somebody's dancing the Watusi in my belly." He sat up. "Bet you don't even know what the Watusi is."

"Something like the minuet," I said, teasing.

He rolled his eyes. "You really know how to hurt a guy. Yesterday at the garage a young kid came in with a jeep and said, 'Hey, old man!'" Dad smirked.

"Well, you should have done the Watusi for him."

"Oh, you don't think I can still do it, eh? Okay, okay, watch this." Dad opened his stereo cabinet and thumbed through his '60s albums. "Here we go. James Brown."

I was laughing now, cinnamon roll crumbs falling out of my mouth.

"That's okay, laugh away. I bet you kids can't dance like this." He put the record on full blast, and I clamped my palms over my ears. Dad started dancing and jumping around the room, waving his arms and bending his knees.

I couldn't stop laughing. "That's the Watusi? You gotta be kidding." I flopped down on a chair to watch.

"Watusi mixed with Monkey," he said. "Try it."

I got up and tried to match his crazy gyrations, but we both ended up laughing so hard at each other that we slumped exhausted onto the sofa. We both sat there panting for a minute and then Dad said, "I think I broke my back."

I looked over at him, and we both burst out laughing again. This was exactly what I needed to soothe my wounds. That afternoon the rain cleared up, and Dad drove me to pick up my car. It looked good as new. Now, to pay for it, I just needed to baby-sit until I turned eighty.

When I got home Sunday night, Mom was out on another date with Dr. Palucci, and it's safe to assume that they were not visiting the arachnid exhibit at the science museum.

There was also a note to call Courtney. I picked up the phone, then put it down again. I didn't want to get all worked up again and start crying. Dad had coached me into feeling really strong and not wanting to get even. I thought about the things he'd said, took a deep breath, then dialed the phone.

Courtney had been feeling light-headed and her vision was blurring lately, so she was lying down in her family room with the sounds of her little brothers zooming around her. "I can't believe you're so calm about this," she said, her voice lowered so her brothers couldn't overhear.

"Well, I was a basket case on Friday," I admitted. "My dad helped me feel a lot better. I should have realized it was an impossible combination—me and Jimmy. Thanks for believing it was real. You didn't even look shocked."

"Oh, please," Courtney said (okay, maybe we don't look alike, but occasionally we *talk* alike). "The only surprise I felt—and this is the truth, Ronnie—is that *you* went for *him*. He doesn't seem smart enough for you. I know he's good-looking, but you would've gotten bored with him."

I was beaming. Courtney always knew exactly what to say. She went on. "You know, you're always putting yourself down, Ronnie. I guess it's because your mom's so, I don't know, glamorous. I wish you could see that you *are* attractive."

Bless her heart. This woman could become President of the United States. What diplomacy. What tact. What utter nonsense. And all spoken without a single chuckle. "C'mon," I said, "I am no babe."

"You just don't see it," Courtney said. "You have a great look, Ronnie. So it isn't like some Vogue model. But it's fresh and honest and full of enthusiasm. You look confident, you look happy, you have great eyes and a great smile."

"Okay, but no autographs," I teased. So could it be true? Were we both girls with skewed perceptions? Courtney imagined herself to be overweight, even though she was emaciated. Was I the victim of delusion, too? Was I seeing myself as plainer than I really was, simply because I paled in comparison to my beautiful mother?

"So what are you going to say to him tomorrow?" Courtney broke into my train of thought.

"I don't know," I said. I had thought of a hundred rude slams, a bunch of lies about Megan Pitney not liking him in the first place, and even telling him I knew his game all along. But Dad's advice kept making my get-even ploys look puny and stupid. "I'll probably just ask him how his weekend went," I said.

Courtney laughed. "I wish I could be as good a sport as you. I'd probably bust up crying."

"Well, I may do that, too."

Mom came home soon and Dr. Palucci—thank heavens—was in a rush and couldn't stay. I was sitting in my bedroom window seat reading when Mom came in. "How are you feeling?" she asked.

"Honestly, Mom, I feel pretty good about everything. I'm relaxed and I feel sorry for him. I really do."

She beamed. "See? *I knew* all you needed was a beauty bath and facial!" She kissed me on the forehead, then glided off to her cozy world of satin sheets and perfumed light bulbs.

14

Butterflies danced the Watusi in my stomach all Monday morning. I took a deep breath before turning the corner into the hall that leads to my English class. Oddly, I discovered I was thinking a silent little prayer. Was God listening? Would he care about one little high schooler's romantic entanglements? I decided he would. I mean, if he's really a Heavenly Father, then he'd be like the ideal dad. And if my own dad cared about my feelings, I knew God would care, too. I asked him to help me be strong.

Luckily, Jimmy wasn't waiting for me in the doorway. I slipped into my seat and got some paper ready to take notes. I kept my hands busy "fixing" my pen and glanced occasionally at the clock. If class would only start without Jimmy in it, I could relax.

Cryson sat at her desk shuffling papers as students drifted in. Maybe she was nervous, like me. Maybe facing a room full of Jimmy Murdock types was a frightening experience.

One minute until class time, and Jimmy still wasn't in his seat. Maybe he broke a leg during his precious football practice. Maybe he woke up covered with acne and was afraid to come to school. Maybe all his hair fell out. I tried to wipe the smile off my face. *Be calm*, I thought.

I screwed my pen back together for the fifth time as Jimmy slid in across the aisle. "Hi!" he whispered.

I forced a cool smile.

"I tried to call you on Saturday—where were you?" He shoved his textbooks under his seat as Cryson stood up.

"I was out dancing the Watusi with an older man," I whispered.

Jimmy looked puzzled and then laughed. He probably thought it was another one of my jokes.

Cryson cleared her throat and saved me from further conversation. "I'm handing your essays back," she said. "Some of you tried to get by with minimum effort this time . . ." she strode down the aisles handing back the papers, ". . . but most of you remembered the exercises we did on description, introduction, and conclusion. Some of your work is very well thought out . . ."

Jimmy's deer-hunting essay smacked down onto his desk top, and I didn't hear another word Cryson spoke. There, in huge, red lettering was a bold "F," about three inches tall. Jimmy grabbed the essay and quickly tucked it under his notebook.

What could possibly have happened? My throat felt dry, and I wondered if Cryson knew that Jimmy had asked me to help him. I closed my eyes, worried sick.

My own essay, a humorous piece about why we should support the space program (so we can send all annoying people to a space station), fell onto my desk. A-minus. Under the grade, Cryson had written, "Please see me after class."

The minutes seemed like hours as I waited to find out what this was all about. I knew Jimmy wasn't a very good writer, but had he changed what I wrote enough to make A-minus work into F work? And if he hadn't touched it, had just handed it in like it was, and if Cryson had known it was my work, why didn't she fail me, too?

Cryson had us open our literature books and begin reading a story by James Thurber. I couldn't concentrate; my eyes just skimmed over the letters without absorbing what they said. Then, she said, "Jimmy, I'd like to speak with you in the hall. Bring your books, please."

I peeked over James Thurber as Jimmy reached under his seat for his books. He didn't see me, but he had a smirk on his face. I quickly went back to my reading.

Soon Cryson returned—alone. Jimmy didn't come back to class. When the bell rang and everyone scooped up their notebooks, I hung back at Cryson's desk. My voice cracked as I said, "You wanted to see me?"

Mrs. Cryson looked over her glasses at me, then walked over

and closed the door. The noise and chatter in the hallway died down. "I think you should know," she said, "that Jimmy will probably be suspended for cheating."

I must have turned white, because she asked me to sit down. "When I read his essay, I immediately suspected that you had helped him. You have a unique writing style, Veronica."

"I was . . . I was just trying to help him. I thought he would use it as an outline. I never meant that he should just hand it—"

"I realize that. It was his choice to use it as an outline, or to turn it in as his own work. That's why I'm not going to punish you. I'm also aware of how Jimmy operates, and I wanted to warn you about him. Veronica, Jimmy was using you. I'm sorry if this is painful to hear, but I can't watch this go any further. I also think you should know about a conversation Mr. Reynolds overheard in the computer lab."

"I think I overheard the same conversation," I said. "With Brad Derrisch?"

Now it was Mrs. Cryson's turn to be surprised. "You already knew?"

It was hard to hold back the tears now, but I blinked them away. "I just found out Friday."

"Veronica, I'm terribly sorry."

"Thank you." I looked out the window, hoping she wouldn't see the tears in my eyes. How many other members of the faculty knew about this?

"Veronica, you did what any girl would have done," Mrs. Cryson said. "I know you're a good student. You drive me crazy sometimes." Then she smiled. She looked like somebody's cuddly grandma at that moment, and I smiled back. "But," she said, "you have great talent. How do you think I recognized your work? Nobody else in this school writes with your unique style."

Now I grinned. This felt so good to hear. "I have a unique style?"

She laughed. "Unmistakable! And a slightly different vocabulary than Jimmy's, too. However," and now she became a teacher again, "if you're serious about journalism, you need to adhere to a higher code of ethics."

I was puzzled. I had always thought I *was* ethical.

"If a handsome newspaper editor asks you to write a story that isn't true . . . or change quotes . . . or anything else that compromises you, what are you going to do?"

I froze, absolutely mortified. Through all my anguish over being duped by Jimmy, I had completely forgotten that I had sold out as a writer. I had written an essay that supported deer hunting, a stance exactly opposite of how I really felt. "Oh, my gosh," I whispered. "I wrote an essay to promote deer hunting."

"And you don't believe a word of it."

I stared at Mrs. Cryson, who had just yanked me into the future. "You're right. I wrote a lie."

She stood up. "You'd better hurry, or you'll be late to your next class."

I was still reeling from the sickening realization that I had been bought. A gorgeous guy had turned my brain to jelly, and here I was, no better than someone who writes an essay about—I don't know, the benefits of pornography, say—simply because it pays well. I was disgusted with myself.

Just as I opened the door, I turned back to Mrs. Cryson. "Thank you," I said. "I can't believe I did that. I'm so sorry—"

She waved me away, smiling again. I walked out of her room ashamed, almost horrified that I could sell out so completely, and for a cretin like Jimmy Murdock. Never, I vowed quietly in my heart, never would I sell out again. A real journalist stays true to her convictions. Besides, Dad was right; I shouldn't have to jump through hoops to get a guy to like me. What kind of dumb premise is that, anyway? Either a guy sees your value or he doesn't. You don't have to manufacture value—it's inborn.

Something felt warm inside, like a spiritual comfort of some kind. I felt certain I was the child of a loving Father in Heaven, and that he really did care about my feelings. Best of all, I felt he was nodding and smiling at my new resolve, and the discovery I'd just made that I was *brimming* with value, if only because I was a daughter of God.

15

"So what happened?" Courtney was leaning close to my ear, whispering.

I smiled as we got in line for lunch, then glanced around to make sure no one was listening. "He's being suspended for cheating," I whispered.

Courtney's jaw dropped. "Get out!"

"That seems to be exactly what they'll tell him."

Now she laughed. "Are you serious? Well, it serves him right."

"It's strange," I said. "I thought I'd be pleased, but I kind of feel sorry for him. I mean, this will knock him off the football team, won't it?"

"Veronica, are you crazy? What do you care? He was *using* you."

"I know, but somehow I feel like I came out ahead. Hey—Cryson recognized my writing."

Courtney smiled. "Oh. Well, so much for my idea to get you to write a report on Herbert Hoover for me." I glanced at her for just a second to see if she was serious, then we both busted up laughing, and sat down to wait for the big news of Jimmy's suspension to spread.

"This is how it's going to be in journalism," I said, trying—unsuccessfully—to cut that day's cafeteria mystery meat. "I'll know some big story, something really hot, and I'll be sitting in a room full of people who won't know a thing about it."

Courtney tore open her milk carton. "I thought journalists wanted to share news."

"Yeah, but not by, like, getting up on a table and shouting it. In this case, I think I'll just let the news travel by itself. But it's weird to know something ahead of everyone else. Like knowing the future or something."

Courtney smiled, thinking about our secret. "Cool."

That afternoon I hurried home, anxious about calling Governor Barrett's secretary again. I hoped she wouldn't tell me to call again in another week. This could go on until I was in college. I dialed the phone. While I listened to it ring, I wondered if I'd have better luck if I hounded her every day. Or maybe I'd just make her mad.

GOVERNOR SIGNS STALKER BILL
Twelfth-Grade Pest Leads to New Law

In an unprecedented move, Governor Barrett today signed into law a bill making it illegal for anyone under 18 to call his office. "We're certain we saw her looking in the windows," Barrett said.

"That girl was relentless," sighed his secretary.

Just then she answered the phone. Stammering, I explained who I was again, and asked if I could schedule an interview with the governor. She put me on hold. *Oh, great*, I thought. *She's probably tracing the call, notifying the police, the FBI—*

"How about Friday?"

I sighed. Another four days of suspense. "You want me to call in the afternoon again?" I asked.

"No—not a phone call," she said, a smile in her voice. "The Governor will *meet* with you on Friday."

My heart leaped up to my eyeballs. "What? Oh! Great! Seriously? Where? When? Seriously?"

She chuckled. "He'll be in your city at the convention center on Friday, and can give you half an hour beginning at two o'clock. Can you be there?"

"Can I be there? Wow—yes! Absolutely! Two o'clock. I'll be there!" My feet were off the ground. I called Mother and she was thrilled. (*Please don't credit this to the cucumber mask*, I thought.) Then I called Dad and I could hear his voice echo through the garage as he whooped and hollered. "Hey, Steve—my kid is gonna interview the governor!" I heard him yell.

Then I called Courtney, who squealed, "Veronica, this is fantastic! You'll be famous!"

Mother came home early and got right on the phone to Uncle Scott and Aunt Mia (who still hadn't entirely forgiven me, but who were chalking most of it up to my being a teenager). I've never seen Mom glow with such pride. "That's right, just like she said she would," Mother gloated. "Friday. Yes, he's giving her the *afternoon.*"

I rolled my eyes.

"Yes," Mother said, "We'll let you know all about it."

The next day at school I got called out of homeroom to see Mr. Emerson. My heart fell, and I knew I'd probably get suspended after all for that horrible deer-hunting fiasco. Jimmy probably gave his side of it, implicating me as the mastermind behind it all. GOVERNOR CANCELS INTERVIEW WITH STUDENT. *Discovers she's a suspended cheating accomplice.* I'd be famous, all right.

My hands were clammy as I sat in the counseling office, waiting to see him. I turned my hall pass over and over in my fingers. Finally he opened the door. "Veronica?"

I stood, wobbly. Mr. Emerson ushered me into his office. What if he knew Gloria and she told him that I said my cat was named Mr. Emerson? I mean, this is a small world and stranger things have happened. I sat down in a cool green leather chair. Was it cold in here, or was I just imagining?

A smiling wife and children sat frozen in their picture frames behind him. He sighed as he lowered his huge body into a gray swivel chair.

"I just wanted to personally congratulate you," he said.

For helping Jimmy Murdock get suspended? Boy, the faculty must really have it in for that poor fool.

"I beg your pardon?" I was hoping he'd be a little more specific.

"We've never had a student interview the governor before," Mr. Emerson said. "I just want you to know we're all very proud."

Ah! My pulse rate dropped by half and I beamed. Thank

heavens for friends like Courtney, who spread the word so well. "Oh, thank you," I said. Whew. Maybe he didn't even know about The Case of the Copied Essay. "I'm really excited. I'll be meeting him on Friday."

"So I hear. We hope you'll tell him hello from Jefferson High."

"Oh, I will. I will."

"We have every confidence that you will be a good representative of our students." It sounded like there was a hint of a directive there. In other words, don't pull anything wild.

"Thank you." *Thank you, Mother, for teaching me to say "thank you" and then button it.*

"You can go back to class now," Mr. Emerson said. "We look forward to reading your interview in the school paper."

"Thank you." I floated back to class, relieved that word of my interview might just overshadow anything *else* he might have heard about me lately.

Eddie Dregman is probably the least gorgeous guy at school. He has orange hair, white eyelashes, yellow freckles, and a skinny neck. He looks like a hybrid squash.

For this reason I invited him over Tuesday afternoon. I figured any guy who looked like Eddie had to have developed the heck out of his personality. (If I could have bought a t-shirt with a red circle and slash line over the picture of a hunk, I would have worn that, too. No more poster boys for me!)

And I was right. He was shy at first and looked at me kind of skeptically when I said, "Hey, Eddie, why don't you come over and we'll make ice cream this afternoon." All right, some of that skepticism could have been because it was the middle of winter. But I think I startled him, too. After all, it was a pretty brazen approach. I just bluntly hit him with the invitation, didn't beat around the bush, and went boldly where no woman had ever gone before.

But being known, as I am, for off-the-wall remarks and jokes, I knew I could always pretend I was kidding if he rejected me outright. That's one nice thing about being outspoken: you can say what you really mean, and then if the entire school laughs at you, you can laugh with them and pretend you weren't serious.

But he squinted his already squinty eyes at me and said, "Okay. You mean you make ice cream—from scratch?"

Ah, yes. *Hard to believe that someone as loaded with looks as I am is also loaded with culinary talent, eh, Eddie?* I didn't say these things, Mother would be glad to know, I just thought them. But, let's face it, what else is a girl like me going to do on the weekends? "Actually, we use cream and ice and berries and some other things. But if you like scratch, I can throw some in."

Eddie chuckled. A good move, Eddie. "So will you come over?" I asked. I felt terribly aggressive. Maybe it was my feeling of confidence after surviving the Jimmy Murdock crash. Or maybe it was from landing the interview with the governor. But also, something told me Eddie would say yes. Here was a guy who wasn't obsessed with girls who have thick, silky hair.

"Sure. I'll be there." And then he *blushed*. I mean, the guy blushed. It was awesome. *So that's how guys feel when girls blush*, I thought. I used to try to blush intentionally into the mirror, after reading in a magazine that men find it attractive. (I have since reconsidered this and decided not to believe everything I read.) But it doesn't matter anyway, because I couldn't do it on cue. The only guy who ever made me blush was Jimmy. For an instant, I wanted to grab him by the sleeve and say, "By the way—all those times I blushed were only because your zipper was down." But Dad was right— Jimmy wasn't worth the trouble.

So now Eddie was blushing. I grinned. I mean, if he was nervous, then he had to care, right? This was going to be great.

I told Courtney that I'd invited Eddie Dregman over for ice cream, and she slammed her brush down on the bathroom counter. "You *what*?" She knew from my expression that I wasn't kidding, either.

"Yep. We're gonna make strawberry and peppermint."

"Oh, gross!"

"Hey, I thought you liked those flavors."

Courtney zipped her purse closed. "I don't mean the ice cream. I mean Eddie Dregman. I mean, what's the deal? You just break up with Jimmy, and now you're asking *Eddie* over?" Sometimes Courtney forgets that she's a diplomacy whiz.

I smiled. "I like him. He's smart."

"True." Now she sighed. "At least you'll have *that* in common."

I grinned and gave her a playful shove. I wish I saw everything in me that Courtney does.

Eddie was exactly on time, and he looked relatively happy for a guy who had just gotten bulldozed into dropping by some girl's house. At school Eddie was always very solemn and serious, but now he almost looked relaxed. And I felt the way he looked—happy and relaxed.

It was weird; around Jimmy I always felt nervous and could never be myself. But with Eddie, it was like he was just a good friend and a fun person. I felt totally comfortable with him. Here was a guy I could honestly trust.

I knew I should probably be embarrassed, or at least uneasy, about inviting him over like I did. But instead, I was delighted with myself.

Eddie got right into things in the kitchen. He helped me measure and stir . . . he was terrific.

"Eddie, you're a good sport," I said.

He laughed. "Sports! That's funny. I don't hear that very often."

"You don't like sports?" This guy was winning my favor fast.

"Well, I like to watch, but I don't play very well," Eddie said.

"Me too." Now it was awkward. I filled in the silence. "What do you like to do?"

"Science. And movies. I really like old movies. And I like to read. I take piano." On and on he went, listing a lot of the same things I like. He even agrees with me that Rocky and Bullwinkle is a classic cartoon and that Woody Allen is obsessed with New York and death. Dad would think it was "far out" that Eddie thinks there's no such thing as a sports car with a Chevy engine. He also thinks fruitcake should be regulated by the Food and Drug Administration as a dangerous substance, and that there is no such thing as a person whose looks improve when they turn their baseball caps around. He agrees with me about almost everything.

I knew my mother would despise him.

I was right. Mother took one look at Eddie's skinny, freckled arms and turned into a frozen goddess. Well, maybe not entirely frozen, but very well chilled. I was surprised that she even wanted some ice cream.

"So. Are you two assigned to the same school project?" Mother was leaving open the possibility that I had been forced to keep company with this homely kid.

Eddie answered for me. "We have taken on the gruesome task of determining which is better—strawberry or peppermint. The peppermint is winning, I think."

I laughed. "No, the strawberry."

"At least we agree that the mixture is losing." Eddie picked up a spoon from the bowl where we had combined flavors, and big globs of pink dripped back into the bowl.

"Yes, that one has definitely pulled out of the race," I said.

Mother smiled one of her Charm School Specials. If Eddie had known her better, he would have quit clowning around. But from his perspective she looked pleasant, even amused. From mine, she looked aghast at the realization that I was with Eddie *by choice*. Her eyes held out some kind of hope that our friendship would end as abruptly as it began, however, and she said, "Well! You two have a good time." Then she disappeared into her home office to work on the fashion show.

"Gee," Eddie said, "I don't know whether to feel flattered or insulted. Obviously your mother trusts me completely."

I laughed, covering my mouth, which was full of peppermint

ice cream. Eddie was wonderful. He was even starting to look a little handsome to me. "Maybe she likes you," I lied.

"Think so?"

I quickly stuffed a spoonful of ice cream into my mouth. "Mmm," I said, letting him interpret that however he chose to.

"She sure is pretty." Well, he could hardly say anything else. I mean, here's this drop-dead gorgeous mother who waltzes in like the Sugar Plum Fairy. I just hoped he wouldn't try to fumble with a comparison of the two of us.

"She runs a modeling agency, right?"

I nodded.

"I guess a lot of girls want to be models," Eddie said.

"Quite a few."

Eddie licked his spoon. "I'm glad you're not a model," he said.

"You are?" This was a new one. I thought all guys preferred models to anything else.

"Yeah," Eddie said. "I think it's cool that you want to be a journalist. I wish I could write. I'd rather eat a whole Christmas fruitcake than write an essay."

I laughed. "Well, anytime you need some help . . ." *Oh, what am I—nuts? Can't I ever learn?*

"You know what I wrote my last paper on?" he asked. "It was on why we should support the space program."

I blanched. "Are you serious?"

"Why—what's the matter?"

"I wrote *mine* on the same thing!"

"So? It's not like they'll think we shared notes, Veronica."

Ha ha ha. Little you know. How long, I wondered, before some faculty member would suspect me of supplying the entire twelfth grade with their essays? "I guess you're right," I said.

Then Eddie elaborated about his paper, explaining all the deep, scientific reasons why we should support the space program. He felt real passion for astronomy, and had strong philosophical arguments. "Was that kind of how your report was, too?" he asked.

I smiled. "Yeah. Kind of."

*   *   *

The next day, Eddie came by my locker and thanked me again for having him over. "Hey, why didn't you tell me you were going to interview the governor?" he asked. "I just heard."

I shrugged.

"That is super exciting," he said. "Way to go."

And then I blushed. "Well . . . it's okay."

"Okay? It's fantastic. And listen, I have some ideas—I mean, you probably already have your questions ready, but I . . . if you'd like to come over after school, I mean, maybe I could help you get ready for the interview. . . ."

"Sure," I said. "I'd love to hear your ideas."

Jimmy who?

I told the car pool to go without me and walked with Eddie to his house. It was really interesting—kind of rustic, with a fireplace in the kitchen and thick beamed ceilings. It felt like a house where you could kick off your shoes and have a pillow fight.

His mom was very quiet and studious-looking. She's an activist for endangered species. His dad had some kind of job in computers, and wasn't home yet. We sat in his family room and devised all kinds of questions for Governor Barrett while we drank soup from thick, glazed mugs. Most of the questions were silly, but we came up with some good current issues to ask about, too. Mrs. Dregman had some excellent ideas (I knew she would the minute I saw her), and within two hours I felt very well prepared.

Mom picked me up on her way home from the studio. I was glad she didn't have her snakeskin boots on.

18

At school Thursday I could hardly pay attention. My nervousness about the interview was really building. It didn't help for every teacher and student (or so it seemed) to keep stopping me in the hall and saying, "Are you nervous?"

By the time school was over, I was ready for a straitjacket. I knew if I kept thinking about Governor Barrett I'd go berserk, so I asked Courtney if I could come over to her place until Mom got home.

On the way there, I thought about how the news of Jimmy's suspension had swept through the school and then died. Hardly anyone even talked about it now. Word was that he wouldn't be able to finish the football season, even after coming back to school in a week. Suddenly the whole studentbody knew his GPA, which—with a failing grade from Cryson—would now dip below the 2.0 mark, a requirement for football players.

At Courtney's house, she changed into leotards and started exercising immediately.

"Oh, Courtney, come on. Give yourself a break. How can you push yourself like this?" She'd been complaining about feeling tired all week, and now she was working out again.

"Yes, Mother," she teased, twisting from the waist with her arms extended like helicopter blades.

"Liftoff. We have liftoff," I mumbled into my fist.

Courtney smiled and kept counting.

"Where are the boys today?" I asked. Usually her brothers were the first home from school, tearing the house to pieces.

"Mom took them to scouts at the church." She puffed as she exercised. "Dad's going to pick them up after work."

"Hey, mind if I turn on the radio?" I asked. Watching Courtney lose even more weight was not my idea of an uplifting afternoon. Courtney mumbled, "Go ahead," and I clicked the power button of the Calhouns' stereo system.

Dr. Palucci! I reached for the channel knob, then changed my mind. Maybe today he'd talk about anorexia and Courtney might learn something. Mom wasn't dating him anymore, so it made it a little easier to listen to him.

But instead of discussing eating disorders, he was talking to some woman whose mother had died ten years ago, and this woman felt bad because she couldn't feel bad. "I've never shed a tear, and I know I ought to," the woman whispered, as if lowering her voice so her deceased mother couldn't hear her.

"How can she not feel bad that her *mother* died?" Courtney asked. I nodded. Even though I get exasperated with my mom, I'd be devastated if I lost her.

Then Dr. Palucci asked what kind of mother she'd had. Courtney and I gasped as the woman went on to tell about the horrendous verbal and physical abuse she had endured as a child. "Sheesh," I said. "No wonder she hasn't cried! She ought to throw an annual fiesta. I say forget about it, and enjoy a long-deserved vacation."

Now Dr. Palucci was whispering back to the caller. "Write your mother a letter. Tell her how angry you are about all the terrible things she did. Then take the letter to her grave and read it to her."

"Oh, give me a break," I said. I'm sure a ten-year-old corpse—or any corpse at all—is going to listen to this woman's letter. What is this—voodoo psychology?"

Courtney laughed. "Shhh."

Spiderman went on. "Tell her everything you've ever wanted to. Then burn the letter and scatter the ashes over the grave. You'll feel better immediately, the tears will come, and you'll be able to finish grieving her death."

"Grieving her *life*," I said. "And the tears will come because the little men in white suits will catch her doing this and take her away."

Courtney was laughing now, begging me to be quiet.

"Seriously," I said. "Everyone who thinks it's legal to start a bonfire in a cemetery, say 'aye.'"

Courtney put her hands over her ears, trying not to laugh and to get back to exercising.

The caller on the radio was sighing now. "Oh, that's beautiful, Doctor. Thank you so much."

I shook my head. "Better yet, get a little doll and stick pins in its head. Then dangle it over an open flame. . . ." I switched off the radio. "C'mon," I said. "Let's go eat and not throw up. You're crazy, you know that?"

"I'm not hungry. I have a headache, anyway."

"Baloney. You look like the Queen of Concentration Camps. Anybody as thin as you *has* to be hungry."

Courtney smiled and checked her watch. "I'll just do twenty minutes more. Stay and talk, okay?"

I sighed, and went into the kitchen to rummage for cookies. Everything said "low fat," which tells you it won't taste worth a flip. When I came back to Courtney, she was jogging in place and doing high kicks. I imagined she would be good at the Watusi. I sat on the sofa and picked up a magazine.

"Eighteen, nineteen," Courtney whispered to herself.

I guess I felt a little sad for that poor woman on the radio. I mean, it must have been a lousy childhood. At least I love my mom. I pictured myself calling old Antonio on the radio and saying, "I love my mother, but she's so gorgeous that I feel like a constant disappointment to her." He'd probably say, "Here's what I want you to do. Take some Coral Frost lipstick and write all your feelings on one of the giant mirrors in her studio. Then wipe it all off with eye makeup remover pads, and the tears will come and everything will be all better."

Just then Courtney started coughing and held still.

"Courtney, are you all right?"

Then suddenly she clasped her chest and doubled over. "Veronic—" she choked and fell hard against the floor, landing in a limp heap.

"Courtney!" I screamed and ran to her, but she had fainted.

"Courtney. Hey!" I squeezed her cheeks and took her hand, but there was no response. "Courtney, c'mon," I said, and rolled her onto her back. Her skin looked pale and pasty.

I put two fingers to the side of her neck and didn't feel a pulse. Her wrist didn't have a pulse, either. "Oh, please," I said, my eyes filling with tears. "Father in Heaven . . ." I knew he was there, even though I didn't pray much. Was he listening?

"Courtney, come on!" I was screaming again, but she just lay there. Remembering the CPR we'd learned in health class, I leaned her head back. Her throat was clear, so I started breathing for her. Her chest filled and lowered, and I climbed on top of her to press her chest. "One, one-thousand, two . . ."

My own chest was pounding as I tried to get a pulse back for her. "Come *on*, Courtney," I said. Finally I heard a beat, or thought I did. "Courtney, please. *Please.*" Suddenly it hit me like a giant, cold hand shaking my shoulders. *Your friend is dying.* Yet it couldn't be happening. It just couldn't be.

I knew I couldn't save her by myself. I called 911, then ran back to Courtney and continued CPR. She seemed so tiny and frail. I was scared I'd break her sternum. And the bones seemed to protrude like a skeleton's.

"Courtney, come on." I was terrified. If only her mother or father would come home. Anybody. Anybody.

Finally I heard sirens, and I tried to swallow with a dry throat as paramedics lifted Courtney onto a stretcher. One of them took over the CPR. Just as they were taking her to the ambulance, Courtney's mother pulled up to the curb. Her face was white as she jumped from the car. "What happened?"

"Courtney collapsed," I said, trembling and stammering.

Everything moved like lightning, and the ambulance driver asked Mrs. Calhoun to follow in her own car. They didn't want her in the ambulance for some reason.

"Please. I want to go, too," I said, and we got into her station wagon. Mrs. Calhoun was crying, almost hysterical. I found myself thrust into the position of having to calm and assure her, when I wanted to fall apart and be comforted myself. But this was Courtney's mom, and I had to stay strong for her.

"They came really quickly," I said.

"Pray, pray," Mrs. Calhoun kept saying. "A cardiac arrest. Oh, Courtney . . ."

I closed my eyes. If praying could pull her through, our prayers would do it. I just couldn't believe this was happening.

19

When Mrs. Calhoun and I arrived at the emergency room, Courtney was already hooked up to what looked like a million tubes and wires. A monitor called an EKG scope was blipping steadily beside her, and when Mrs. Calhoun saw it she grabbed my arm and said, "Look! Her heart is beating—thank heavens."

Courtney had a tube in her nose and an intravenous tube in each arm. A doctor was injecting something straight into the tube on one of them. Somebody said something about her being on a ventilator, and Mrs. Calhoun asked a nurse if Courtney was breathing on her own.

"Not yet," the nurse said. "My name is Georgia Minton. Can you tell me what happened?"

Mrs. Calhoun looked as lost as anybody I've ever seen. She looked over at me, her eyes still pools of tears, and waited for me to answer.

"Courtney was exercising," I said. "Doing kicks and things, and she collapsed."

"How long ago?" The nurse was scribbling on a clipboard.

"About twenty minutes."

"Did you notice any jerking movements?"

"No, none."

A doctor behind her said, "B-P is only sixty by palpation. Start a dopamine drip."

Mrs. Calhoun became pale and the nurse helped her to a chair. "That's just something for the blood pressure," the nurse said.

"Give her some soda bicarb . . ." I could hear the doctor saying,

". . . some epinephrine, that's right . . ."

"She wears contacts," I told one of the nurses.

"My baby, my baby." Mrs. Calhoun was crying and Nurse Minton sat beside her, a strong-looking arm around Mrs. Calhoun's shoulders.

"It's all right," the nurse was saying. "We're doing everything possible. I need some more information."

Mrs. Calhoun tried to regain some composure. I felt as if I was sinking in quicksand. I couldn't begin to imagine what a mother must be feeling. Everything seemed to rush by in a blur, yet nothing was moving fast enough. *Help her, help her,* I kept thinking. *Do it faster, get her going* now!

"Has she had any health problems?" Nurse Minton asked.

"We've suspected anorexia," Mrs. Calhoun said. "She's seen a counselor for it. She throws up after her meals sometimes, but I never thought it could lead to this!" Courtney's mom was crying and shaking now, completely dissolved.

I sat beside her, then turned to the nurse. "She's been tired. And she told me she's been having heart flutters, but we both thought it was just nervousness. And headaches. And she was dizzy."

"Her eyes," said Mrs. Calhoun. "She's had blurred vision this week."

The whole weight of Courtney's collapse seemed to come down on me as I quietly blamed myself for not doing something sooner. She had been so tired, and I had thought she simply needed to eat more. Finally, I couldn't talk; I only cried along with Mrs. Calhoun.

"My daughter needs a priesthood blessing," Mrs. Calhoun said. "Can I call my husband?"

"I can do that for you, if you wish," the nurse said.

Mrs. Calhoun pulled a business card from her purse, then wrote a second number on the back. "And my bishop."

The nurse took the card and stepped away to a phone.

"What's a priesthood blessing?" I asked Courtney's mom.

Suddenly Mrs. Calhoun looked incredibly strong. "It's using the actual power of God to heal someone," she whispered. Her words were soft, but they thundered right through me. That was one of the theories I'd always had about religion—that it ought to tap in directly to God, not just be something men created by committee.

"How does someone do that?" I asked.

"The power of the priesthood is what Jesus used when he was on the earth," Mrs. Calhoun explained. "It's given by the laying on of hands to worthy men in Christ's church. It's the authority to ordain, to even perform miracles." She sighed, seemingly unsure about how much of this I understood. "Veronica, we believe our church is the exact church Christ organized in ancient days. It was lost, and that's what makes Mormons different from everyone else. We believe his actual church was restored in modern times—with that same priesthood authority. We have a living prophet, apostles, all the same ingredients as the original church. And men who hold that power, which we call the priesthood, can heal the sick."

I stared for a minute, then whispered, "Awesome!" So *that's* what Mormons believed. And all this time I thought it was just a bunch of rules like not dating before you're sixteen, and not smoking or drinking. Why hadn't Courtney told me all this? This was totally cool, totally logical. No wonder there was so much splitting off and fighting in the early Christian churches. Of *course* the real McCoy had to be restored.

My mind was spinning. I'd never felt such intense emotions in my life. Was I in shock? I felt such horror and panic for Courtney, yet my soul was spinning and leaping at these new ideas. How could I contain such intense feelings? And, amazingly, the things Mrs. Calhoun was saying seemed to be calming both of us, giving us what—faith? It felt as if someone was trying to hug me, but couldn't quite reach.

Dr. Thurman, a wiry, intense man, looked up at us, then said to another nurse, "Get a minor panel. Let's check that potassium. Get her ABGs, too." Then he came over to us. "Nobody's to blame here, all right? Apparently her electrolytes were way off and she got dehydrated. I think that's what caused the arrest. We're doing our best." Then he nodded at me. "Congratulations for doing CPR, young lady. You kept her alive until help arrived. You can be very proud of yourself."

I cried harder for some reason, and Mrs. Calhoun hugged me. "Thank you, Veronica," she whispered.

We watched the flurry of activity around Courtney, then Dr. Thurman stepped away to speak to us again. "We won't know if she's going to recover completely until she comes around. She's still critical, but the prognosis looks good. If she wakes up during the next twenty-four hours, she probably won't have any residual effects."

"You mean brain damage." Mrs. Calhoun looked bravely back at him.

Dr. Thurman sighed. "Yes. It's a possibility."

"And she might not . . ." Mrs. Calhoun couldn't say it, but we all thought it: Courtney might not wake up.

"Don't think of that side. Hope and pray for the best." Then Dr. Thurman returned to Courtney.

"I'd better call my mother," I said. Nurse Minton advised me to stay seated, at which moment I suddenly noticed I was still shaking. "Thank you," I said, giving her Mom's studio number. "Please tell her I'd like to stay here all night with the Calhouns." Then I turned to Courtney's mom. "If that's all right."

She held me close. "Of course."

Another nurse came in soon, and told Dr. Thurman that Courtney's potassium was 2.2. Mrs. Calhoun looked helpless and worried sick, so I said, "2.2—that's good, Mrs. Calhoun." Of course, I had no idea whether it was good or not, but I felt I had to say something encouraging; Courtney's mom looked so lost.

Mr. Calhoun and the boys, Zack and Trevor, charged into the room. Mr. Calhoun's face was streaked with tears, and the two boys were pale as cream. Dr. Thurman repeated what he had said to us and told them that my CPR had kept Courtney alive.

Again, that made me cry. I guess I was just so tremendously grateful that I had known what to do. And I was so glad I'd been able to do *something*, however small. I shuddered to think what might have happened if I hadn't gone to her house after school.

Nurse Minton came over to me. "Your mother said it's fine for you to stay here. And she said to remind you about the governor."

Barrett—I'd forgotten completely. I'd simply have to cancel. My best friend could be dying; this was no time to be leaving her side, no matter what.

"Can I use your phone to call his office?" I asked. It was almost

5:00; perhaps his secretary would still be there. The nurse offered to call for me, but I felt I should explain this myself.

Luckily, the secretary was in, and she seemed very understanding when I explained what had happened to Courtney. I told her that interviewing the governor was the greatest honor I could imagine, but that I wanted to stay with my friend in case she became conscious for a few minutes. I was sure Barrett would think I was another flaky kid, but I didn't care. If there was a chance—any chance at all—that Courtney could know it, I wanted her to know I was at her side.

When I came back, the Calhouns' bishop had arrived and was with them in Courtney's room. He and Mr. Calhoun seemed to be praying over her with their hands on her head. I sat in the lounge to wait.

I'd read somewhere that people can sense when they're abandoned, even when they're in a coma. Also, the last sense to go (and the first to return) is hearing. I wanted to talk to Courtney, maybe say something that would give her some hope. But only her parents were allowed to be close to her in the emergency room; the rest of us had to wait a few hours.

"Why don't you go home and get some rest?" Mrs. Calhoun asked as she came out of Courtney's room. "You can come back later."

I glanced at Zack and Trevor. If I stayed and watched them, it would free up both of Courtney's parents to be with her—and with each other. "I want to stay with the boys," I said. Again, Mrs. Calhoun gave me a hug.

Zack, just eight years old, tried to be such a brave little man, clenching his teeth and blinking back the tears. Trevor, five, cried into my lap like a baby. Finally I pulled Zack over and he wept along with us. Though nothing was said, we all tried to dry our tears occasionally and be strong for each other. It was amazing how much we communicated without speaking.

I kept wondering about Courtney's blessing, but didn't want to pry about something sacred if it was private. Finally I cleared my throat and got up the nerve to ask. "Mrs. Calhoun?"

She had been sitting on the sofa with me, staring into space.

Now she looked over at me. "Yes?"

"What was that blessing Mr. Calhoun gave Courtney? Do you mind if I ask?"

She smiled and stroked my hair. "Of course not, honey. When a man who holds the authority to do it lays his hands on someone's head, he can actually heal them." And then she bit her lip, blinking back the tears. "It was beautiful. Courtney was promised a full recovery," she said. "And," she added, taking a breath, "she is to be an example to others, to help them overcome this terrible disorder."

I swallowed, amazed that something akin to miracle-working had been done just a few yards from where I was sitting.

Other emergencies punctuated the evening, sometimes accompanied by a little cluster of horrified relatives whose chances to say "I love you" had suddenly been cut short. I thought about how hard it was to tell my mom and dad that, and I resolved to find a way.

At least a dozen people from Courtney's church came by to assist with blessings, bring sandwiches, and lend moral support.

By ten o'clock that night they said Courtney's condition had stabilized, and now they could move her to the intensive care unit. Courtney's regular doctor, Dr. Brault, had been in. Dr. Thurman also called in a cardiologist and a neurologist. When we found Courtney's new room, two women were talking at the foot of her bed. "Potassium's 2.9 now," one was saying, and the other, a doctor, told her to repeat some lab tests.

There was a waiting room for the family—it was assumed I was part of that—and they said we could each go in separately to visit Courtney, if we wanted. I waited for her family to take their turns, then went in last.

The doctor and nurse were back in again. "I understand you're Veronica," the doctor said. "My name is Evelyn Fletcher. I'm a cardiologist."

"How do you do," I said, and shook her hand.

"You did a fine job on CPR. Did you learn that in school?"

"In health class. They offered it to anyone who wanted to take it. I'm sure glad I did."

"We all are. Would you like to be alone with Courtney? She's still in a coma, you know."

"I would. Can I ask something?"

Dr. Fletcher looked tired, but there was great kindness in her eyes.

"If she's breathing and her heart is beating, why doesn't she wake up?"

"That's a good question. Let me explain. Courtney has hypoxic encephalopathy. This means her brain has been temporarily damaged by the lack of oxygen which occurred immediately after her cardiac arrest. This causes swelling in the brain, and that in turn causes a coma. We expect—and hope—that she'll come out of it in the next day or two."

I looked over at Courtney's emaciated little shell and the tubes feeding life into her body. My eyes burned with tears again. "She will. She has to. She just has to."

20

After the doctor and nurse left, I sat down in a chair beside Courtney's bed. "Hi, buddy," I whispered. My voice wavered and I cleared my throat. "It's Veronica. Everybody says you're going to be all right."

The heart monitor left a green after-image of bleeps on the screen as it kept quiet pace in the darkness. "Everyone's really nice here," I said. "They seem to know what they're doing. I mean, of course, right?" I stopped for a minute and thought about how silly I felt, talking into the stillness. Maybe she couldn't even hear me. But if there was any chance, I wanted to talk some more. I wanted to say things I hadn't ever bothered to say before. "Courtney, you're the best friend I ever had. I love you, and I'm so glad we know each other." I stopped for a moment until the tears subsided. "Hey," I said. "How come you never told me what you Mormons believe? Your mom was just telling me, and it sounded awesome. How come you've been keeping such a cool secret?"

I tapped on the side of the bed, thinking and wondering what to say next. "Hey, when you threw yourself on top of me when they were making that commercial," I reminded her, "I said I owe you one. Now you have to get well so I can pay you back."

Then I went over what seemed like a million other memories with her. "Remember that time in home ec when Krista McNess stuck herself in the fanny with a seam ripper? And ol' Mrs. Bloom ran screaming down the hall for the school nurse? Then Krista was so embarrassed she hid in the ironing board closet? Remember that? And she knocked over the refill bottle for the spray starch, and it ran all over Melissa Weinfeld's tennis shoes? And then—"

A nurse laid her hand on my shoulder. "Veronica, Mrs. Calhoun would like to come in now."

"Oh—oh, sure!" I jumped up, embarrassed. I'd been blabbing away for half an hour. I looked down at Courtney; she was still unresponsive. I touched her. "Courtney, we've all been praying for you, so you have to pray, too, okay?"

Mrs. Calhoun squeezed my hand and we traded places.

In the waiting room, Trevor had fallen asleep, but Zack and Mr. Calhoun were praying. I sat down quietly and closed my eyes, praying along with them.

I couldn't sleep; I just kept staring at different points in the waiting room. There was a tall, stainless steel ashtray with sand in the top. I memorized every dip and crevice in the sand. On the wall hung a landscape of some trees and a path; over and over I studied the brush strokes. I even counted the holes overhead in the acoustical ceiling. Time dragged on and on, every breath accompanying the hope that Courtney would regain consciousness. I refused to imagine her dying. The possibility of attending her funeral occurred to me for a second, but I pushed the thought away immediately.

By three in the morning, the Calhouns were all dozing and I was still wide awake. I tiptoed back into Courtney's room, where everything looked the same as before. Courtney always liked my jokes, and I figured she was hearing enough serious talk—if she was hearing at all.

It was hard to be funny when I thought about how critical her condition was, but somehow I believed she would pull through. And if she could hear me talking to her just like old times, maybe she'd have hope and make it.

"Courtney, I know you haven't opened your eyes yet," I said, "so let me tell you about your room." I described everything for her in a funny way. "There's probably a bedpan around here, I'm sure you'll be thrilled to know," I said. "And there's a painting that looks like it was stolen from a cheap motel. Some people take soap, towels . . . I guess this proves that some people take lousy artwork, huh?" I looked over at the door. "You know, your night nurse looks like Mr. Grimes in drag." Mr. Grimes is one of the P.E. coaches. "Give him a brown wig, white spongy shoes and tube of pink lipstick, and you have Courtney Calhoun's night nurse."

Her breathing stayed steady. "This hospital is really gorgeous," I whispered. "All decorated in white-on-white. Your favorite." Courtney detests white for some reason. I guess she sees it the same way I see plain vanilla ice cream: naked without hot fudge.

"And the food. Oh, Courtney. Such an array of gourmet selections in the cafeteria! I found a new alternative to frosting: Glue! Seriously, you just spread it over a cake and away you go. A little sticky, but . . . hey. You want lower calories or not? We could create a new game show every night. People would line up in the cafeteria line to guess what everything is. It's worse than school, and *as you know*, that's saying something." Once in awhile Courtney and I copy a quirk of a frequent math sub—this lady who says *as you know* throughout her lectures.

"Hey, I came up with a new idea while I was sitting here. I was thinking about Jimmy Murdock and how he used my essay. Probably he's cheated off my test papers, too. So I had this thought. Picture some guy in a TV commercial, Courtney." Then I lowered my voice. "People stealing your ideas? Get *The Brain Club*." I waited, as if she could respond. "What do you think? Can't you just see it—this big pipe you attach to your head!"

Finally I ran out of steam. There was plenty more to joke about, but I found I just wasn't strong enough to keep the act going. I went back out to the waiting room. I was so terribly frightened for her. What if she died? What if she had brain damage? It was all too much, so I went back out to the waiting room. But I still didn't sleep for the rest of the night.

In the morning I called Dad and Mom both, wishing I could report some progress, but so far Courtney hadn't flinched a muscle.

"When do you want me to pick you up for the interview?" Mother asked.

"Oh—I canceled it. I forgot to tell you—"

"Veronica, why on earth did you *cancel?*"

I tried to explain, but Mother just said I was being self-destructive and trying to fail. I think she's been listening to too much Dr. Palucci. It's bad enough to be analyzed by a stranger on the radio, but a modeling instructor?

"I just want to support Courtney," I said. "It's what friends are for. Mom, she needs me. She does."

"Don't be ridiculous. You don't need to prove anything if she's really your friend."

"I *want* to stay with her. When she's eighty-five years old, I want her to remember that when she was seventeen and in the hospital, one of her friends was always at her side."

I could almost hear Mother roll her eyes. "You can still care about her and interview the governor, darling. It would only take a few minutes, then you can go right back."

"It would take an entire afternoon by the time we drive there and wait for him and talk to him and drive back. What if she becomes conscious for a few minutes and I miss it?"

Now Mother sounded angry. "You're throwing away a once-in-a-lifetime opportunity."

And I was *taking* another. Why couldn't she see that I was making the right choice? Besides, I was in no condition to interview anybody, as upset and sleepless as I'd been. No way could I leave Courtney.

"You'll be disappointing a lot of people," Mother said.

So that was it. Mia's dare. All the friends she'd told. I fought the tears. Why couldn't she love me as I was? Why did I have to be winning awards or getting applause to make up for not being like her? Why couldn't she be glad I was a good friend?

"What about your schoolwork?"

"I can catch up," I said. I'd only miss Friday's assignments. Probably Eddie could help me.

"How are you eating?"

I told her I had my purse and plenty of money. Besides, people from the Calhouns' church seemed to arrive around the clock with food.

"Well, tell Courtney's family how concerned I am, and that I'm hoping everything will go well," Mother said.

At two o'clock that afternoon, a nurse went into Courtney's room and shouted out into the hall, "She's bucking on the tube!"

We all jumped to our feet. Mr. Calhoun ran to the nurse's

station. "What happened? Is she all right?"

We were right behind him, our faces full of worry. Quickly another nurse seemed to be patting us all on the back at once. "Don't worry," she said. "It's a reflex. It means she's breathing on her own. That's great news."

We all sort of stood there in one giant, sobbing hug, then Mr. and Mrs. Calhoun asked to see her.

Dr. Thurman was there immediately and removed the endotracheal tube. At four o'clock we were all in the waiting room when Dr. Fletcher came in. "We have some good news," she said. "Courtney is regaining consciousness."

Mrs. Calhoun let out a cry of joy, and the rest of us clutched each other in grateful hugs.

"She's lapsed back into a coma again, but I don't want you to worry. That's normal. Regaining consciousness is a series of small steps."

A wave of tremendous relief swept over us all, and the two boys slumped happily into their chairs.

At five o'clock she awoke again, but was confused and didn't know where she was or what had happened. By six-thirty, she knew her parents and seemed oriented pretty well. Then she drifted off to sleep again. "We're out of the woods, Veronica," Dr. Fletcher said, "if you'd like to go home."

"Are you sure? I mean, she's definitely going to make it?"

"Definitely. I want to transfer her to the sub-acute ward for a couple of days. We'll need to run some tests. But everything's going to be fine."

The Calhouns decided to stay until ten, but they encouraged me to go home, so I called Mom to come and get me. She met me in the lobby. "I'm so glad Courtney's going to pull through this," she said. "And see? You could have interviewed the governor after all."

I was so furious at that remark that I didn't even respond. The last thing on my mind was the interview with Barrett. Here was Courtney, on the verge of dying, and I had a chance to be at her side. I wouldn't have traded it for anything.

When we got home, Mother's teaching manuals were spread out on the table, some loose pages showing where to determine your foundation color ("under the jawline on the neck; your hand and wrist do not show true skin tone"). There were little squares of color all down the side of the sheet, as if to say, "See? These are the colors of humans. Which one are you?" And, of course, none of them looked like *my* color. They must have been made by the same color-blind folks who brought us party pink Band-Aids.

Mom had an easel propped up, displaying huge photos of a student's makeover. I noticed the "after" picture had been shot with a soft-focus lens. Have you ever seen makeovers in magazines? Ever notice how they always pick people with great bone structure? They may have shaggy hair, flat lips, squinty eyes or a fat neck, *but they will always have dynamite cheekbones.* That's so they'll look 100 percent better, even if all you do is shade their faces right.

"What about your homework? Don't you and that red-haired fellow have to turn in your project soon?"

"That red-haired fellow has a name," I said.

She smiled. "Yes, I know he does. I'm sorry."

I ought to run off with Eddie, marry him, and give her average-looking grandchildren. "You know, he really is a nice guy, Mom. I mean, give me some credit."

She smiled again. "I think it's fine that you're friends with Eddie." Underscore *friends.* "You know, darling, if you're trying to make Jimmy jealous, I don't think this will work."

I laughed. "I wouldn't waste my spit on Jimmy."

"Don't be vulgar, Veronica. That sounds like your father talking."

I just smiled. There was no use explaining why I liked Eddie, or how he suddenly seemed a giant compared to Jimmy. And there was no use explaining why I had passed up the chance to interview the governor. It was going to be a feather in her social cap, and now I had taken that away.

Some of the kids at school had acted the same way, suddenly turning friendly because this business with Barrett had suddenly boosted me up the social ladder.

That was another thing about Eddie that I liked. He was happy for me when I landed the interview, but he liked me before. And I knew he'd still like me now that everything was off. I knew Eddie would agree with the decision I'd made to stay at Courtney's side. I wished he would call.

And then, as if by magic, the phone rang. "I'll get it," I said. "It's probably that red-haired fellow with an update on our project." I picked up the phone.

"Hello, Veronica? This is Janice Montease, Governor Barrett's secretary. I explained your situation to him, and he was so impressed with a friendship like that, that he'd like to fly you to the state capitol to meet with him in two weeks. That is, if your friend is well enough that you can leave her."

21

My whole life seemed to click into fifth gear after that. I felt like I was speeding down a raceway while the whole world whipped by in a blur. Yet I felt in control. It was, as Mother might say, simply mah-velous.

Mother was nearly as thrilled as I was, and since she hadn't told anybody about my canceling the interview, she didn't have to make any embarrassing calls to Scott and Mia.

Dad was not only happy about my interview, he was proud that I had stayed with Courtney. "You did the right thing, Ronnie. And see? That old Barrett wants to meet *you* now. When you shake his hand, you shake it good and hard. Maybe some of your class will rub off on him."

We laughed, then reminisced a bit about his crazy Watusi dancing. I told him about Jimmy getting suspended, and I even told him about Eddie. Despite his not wanting *any* boy to be interested in me, he had to admit that Eddie sounded pretty cool.

When I called Eddie, who had heard the rumors about Courtney at school, he backed me up completely. In fact, he assumed that's where I'd been all along. And when I told him my interview with the governor was on again, he said, "Hot dog!"

"Hot dog?" I laughed. "Eddie, you're weird."

"Too many old movies," he admitted.

"Hey, I think I'll stay with Courtney on Monday, too. Could you explain to my teachers and get the homework for me?"

"It's a done deal. You want me to bring you anything tomorrow so you can study on the weekend?"

"Umm . . . yeah. A chocolate shake and some fries."

Now Eddie laughed. We agreed to meet at the hospital at two o'clock, when visiting hours began. Eddie said he'd try to bring all the class notes he could round up. For Courtney, too.

The next day, just before Mother dropped me off at the hospital, she said, "Remember this is a hospital, Veronica. Don't be boisterous."

I waited for Eddie in the parking lot, and a few minutes later he pulled up on his bike. "Here you go," he said, lifting two chocolate shakes out of a white sack in his backpack. We sat on a bench outside the hospital and drank shakes until two, when we could visit Courtney.

She was asleep when we got there, so we went over schoolwork in the lounge. Mom came back with the Calhouns, and we all visited until the nurses said Courtney was awake. Her family went in first, then Mom and I.

Courtney still had an I.V. in one arm, so I hugged her carefully. "That was some scare you gave us," I said, holding her as tightly as I dared.

She smiled and started to cry. "Veronica, thank you so much. You stayed with me the whole time, didn't you?"

I nodded. More tears. "Wouldn't have missed it."

Courtney dabbed at her eyes. "I'm feeling a lot better. Kind of shook me up."

I grinned and pulled up a chair. "Well, you're gonna be great. And more good news—I brought you some homework."

"Ugh. Thanks a lot."

We all chatted about the hospital food, the care she was getting, the prospects for going home, what the extra tests she was having were for.

"Will you be able to be in the fashion show?" Mom asked. I cringed. How long had she waited to ask that—five minutes?

"Oh, yes—the doctors say I'll be back at school in a week."

We chatted some more, and Mom finally left. I stuck my head out and smiled at Eddie. He seemed content to read a book while I visited with Courtney alone.

"You look good," I said. This wasn't true, but I knew it meant a lot to Courtney to hear it.

"I've got a long way to go." She started to cry again, and I handed her a Kleenex. "I was really lucky. I could have died. You saved my life, Veronica."

Silent tears streaked both our faces, and when we both blew our noses in unison, we laughed. "I've really learned a good lesson, Veronica. I honestly want to get well again. It's going to take me some time, but I desperately want to stop losing weight and being so dumb."

"You're not dumb."

"Yes I am. I gave myself a cardiac arrest."

I smiled. "Okay, maybe a little dumb."

She laughed. It was so *good* to see that. "You know what I want to do? I want to use this experience to help other anorexic girls. I wish I could warn every one of them about what they're doing. Lots of girls at school are bulimic, you know."

"Well, it's the guys," I said. "You look at some of those jerks, and . . ." then I pretended to be gagging.

Courtney laughed again. "Honestly. I mean, I know I still need help myself, but I really want to help them."

"You will," I said. "I know you. And they need it." I looked at the resolve in her eyes. "Look at you," I said. "Here you are, flat on your back in a hospital, and all you can think about is helping somebody else." I really admired her.

"Yeah, and here you are, ready to interview Governor Barrett, and you spend the night in a hospital instead."

"Hey—you're more important than he is. And guess what— he's flying me to the capitol in two weeks to do the interview after all."

Courtney brightened. "Wow! That's fantastic, Veronica. I'm so glad."

"One problem, though. He wants to see me the same Saturday as your fashion show. I had really wanted to be there to watch you."

Courtney waved away my concern and rolled her eyes. "There'll be others. Thank goodness I didn't blow everything for you."

I rubbed her arm, so happy she was alive.

"Is your mom going with you?" she asked.

"Are you kidding? She's been working on that fashion show for months! And anyway, I'm just flying up in the morning and back that afternoon. She can drop me off at the airport, do her show, and pick me up later."

Courtney nodded, then suddenly started laughing. "You know," she said, "my night nurse *does* look like Mr. Grimes in drag!"

I laughed with her and shook my head. Then I stopped. "Hey—Courtney—you heard me say that? You heard me say that!"

She nodded and we hugged, both of us crying like babies all over again. "You heard me; I *knew* you could hear me!" To heck with being boisterous.

"And I owe you an apology," Courtney said, growing serious. "I should have told you about my church a long time ago."

I hugged her. "You don't need to apologize," I said.

"Yes, I do. I had the greatest thing in the world, and I didn't share it with my own best friend."

"You took me to some dances and stuff."

"But I didn't tell you about what we believe."

"It's okay."

"No, it's not," Courtney said. "That's what friends are for, and I should have had more courage. I guess . . . I'm not making excuses, but I guess I never talked about it because I didn't want it to wreck our friendship if you thought I was being too pushy or something."

I nodded. "But it's so logical," I said. "It's exciting."

Courtney smiled. "They call it 'the thinking man's religion.' I should have known you'd like it!"

I laughed. "I don't suppose I'm the easiest person to share stuff like that with. I tend to be . . ." I searched for the word I wanted, thumbing through choices like "overanalytical" and "cynical." "Don't help me here," I warned Courtney.

She laughed. "You're skeptical," she said anyway. "I wasn't sure religion was even something that appealed to you."

I smiled. It was true; we had never talked about anything spiritual. And now, suddenly, nothing fascinated me more.

22

On Sunday, a physical therapist helped Courtney begin walking and getting her strength back, then the next day they let her go home. I wanted to see her on Monday as much as possible, but I didn't want to intrude on the Calhouns' family time, or wear Courtney out.

"Oh, don't give that another thought," Mrs. Calhoun said. "You're her best medicine. We all feel so blessed that you're Courtney's friend."

"Hey," Courtney said, almost sounding as bold as I did when I invited Eddie over. "How would you like to take the missionary discussions?"

My eyebrows went up and I left them there for a few seconds. "The what?"

Mrs. Calhoun smiled at Courtney, then glanced nervously back at me.

Courtney settled into a love seat. "Lessons about the Mormon church," she said.

I smiled. "Uh. Okay. I mean, why not?"

Mrs. Calhoun seemed to be searching for the right words. "Please don't feel obligated, Veronica. You won't upset Courtney if you say no—"

"No, I'd like to do this," I said. "So far, it sounds pretty interesting."

"You're going to get baptized?" Zack asked, his eyes round with excitement. And who, I later learned, had just been through the experience himself.

"Well, that will be Veronica's own decision," Mr. Calhoun said. "If she chooses to, she'll need her parents' approval."

"Of course," Mrs. Calhoun said, wanting to be very careful about all of this.

"Oh, please," Courtney said, sounding as if she'd never even been in the hospital. "Have you ever seen anyone try to stand in Veronica's way?"

I laughed, eager to see what these lessons were all about.

The Calhouns insisted I run it by my parents first. Mother was all for it—said it might have a "softening" effect on me. Ha ha. Dad was quiet for a minute, then said, "Go for it, honey. And let me know the minute you make a decision." That was a little odd, I thought, but I was grateful for his permission.

Even though it was their day off, two missionaries came and taught me that night. Courtney sat in on the discussions, beaming the whole time. When the two men (Elders? Elder than whom?) asked me if I had any questions, the only one I could think of was, "How can you sit here and keep your mind on your work when the beautiful Courtney Calhoun is smiling at you?" But I didn't ask that; I just clarified the basics of their teachings. So far, according to my own deductions, these guys were right on track. This was the religion I felt I had invented in my own head years ago—it had everything I liked in it. For one thing, you can stay married after death. I've always found it creepy to hear marriage ceremonies say "til death do you part." If you've spent a whole lifetime in love with someone, why would you want it to come to a bitter, screeching halt? How can you stop loving someone just because they die? And wouldn't you want your husband and kids with you in the next life? How else could it be heaven?

Another thing I liked was what they called the Word of Wisdom—a health regulation. Courtney started crying and admitted she hadn't been taking care of her body, and said she was determined to repent and change. Instead of it being this list of things you couldn't do, it turned out to be a whole plan of getting enough sleep, eating the right foods, and other good advice. What I liked best was that their prophet received revelation about it a hundred years before anyone even suspected tobacco and alcohol could ruin your health.

"This revelation stuff," I said. "Does it only come to your prophet?"

The missionaries told me that revelation for the Church as a whole only comes through the prophet, but that every person is entitled to his own individual revelation for his own special needs. Wow! No wonder I heard the warning that Courtney was dying. And that feeling of someone trying to reach out and hug me—was that a special communication just for me, too? I could see where a loving Father in Heaven would absolutely plan things so that you're not floundering alone without specific help. Then they told me that this "personal revelation" would be how I could get the answer to my prayers, and know if their church was really the one Christ had set up.

They gave me a Book of Mormon, and asked me to read it and pray about whether it was true. I thumbed through it, wondering how on earth a person could ever know. But I said I'd read it, and that night I began.

About twenty pages into it, I thought I'd kneel down and pray. Almost instantly I felt that hugging thing again. What was I expecting? A vision? Fireworks? Somehow the word "patience" kept trying to penetrate my thoughts. Patience? Patience for what?

And then I realized. I needed patience in my entire life. Here I was, racing through my youth, breaking my neck to get all grown up and make my mark in the world of journalism. The last thing I was, was patient.

It was as if that one little word took on layers and layers of meaning. I needed to be patient with myself, with my mother, with all my classmates. I needed to be patient about religion. I was approaching it like buying life insurance—"Lay out what you have to offer, and let's decide this thing in twenty minutes."

I needed more patience. And so I read. And kept reading. Finally it was one o'clock in the morning, and I figured I could either set a Guiness record for least sleep in a one-week period, or I could get some rest. I remembered the Word of Wisdom; rest was definitely in there.

I took the book to school and kept reading during snatches of free time. The Joseph Smith story—about a fourteen-year-old boy who prayed to know which church to join, and then saw Heavenly Father and Jesus in a vision—at first seemed wildly impossible. But then, as I considered the various options God had for restoring Christ's original church, again I was struck by the logic of it. Who better to oversee the newly restored church than a young man who had been trained from his youth in what to do? And if you have to physically *give* the priesthood power to someone, then you have to cross the barrier between this life and immortality—heavenly beings have to appear to someone. Surely God, who could do anything, could appear to his chosen prophet. I mean, prophets in the Old Testament saw the Lord, right? Why should those people be more privileged than modern ones?

I stepped into the rest room to pray. It was the same rest room where I had cried over Jimmy Murdock, and I deliberately chose the same stall. It may not seem like a spiritual setting, but it was the only private place in school. And instead of feeling anguish and despair, this time I felt peace and assurance. When I prayed about the Joseph Smith story, I felt warm and wonderful. Suddenly the tears I had shed over Jimmy seemed insignificant—little specks, something belonging to earth and mortality. I had come full circle. The new tears I felt were tears of strength and gratitude. I was finding my Savior, my God again. And I knew it was *again*, because I sensed so strongly that I already knew them, and had been with them before my birth. The hug was almost reaching me.

My mind was spinning. I floated through the day, almost oblivious to the clusters of kids who were gathering around me, asking a million questions about Courtney and the hospital. Every time class would start, I felt relieved to be out of the hubbub in the halls.

Ms. Lewis, the health teacher, asked me to come into her class next week for a special CPR demonstration. Mr. Elkin made me stand up while he told all the other kids I was a heroine. It really embarrassed me, but instead of teasing me, all the kids clapped and cheered. Mr. Gomez, the school paper advisor, asked me to write an article about my experience.

And again, I got summoned to Mr. Emerson's office. "Well, well," he said. "We're getting to be old friends."

I smiled, and prayed that he would never hear about my cat,

my connection to Jimmy Murdock, or Eddie's space program essay.

"You're an amazing young lady," he said. "Full of surprises."

Little did he know.

"We're proud of you. A real heroine."

I could feel my cheeks burning. "Anyone else would have done the same," I said.

He shook my hand. "Maybe. Maybe not. The important thing is that you did it. I commend you."

"Thank you. Well, guess I'll scoot back to class."

"Wait. I got a call from Channel Four. They want to interview you."

"What?"

Mr. Emerson scribbled a name and number on a piece of paper for me and said I could use his phone. I gulped and picked up the receiver. How many times had he spoken into this very gadget to tell my parents I needing "reining in"? And now, here I was, the toast of the town.

I spoke to the assignments editor, and he asked if he could send a camera crew to my house that very evening. "Uh, sure," I said. "Would you like me to write a story about it?" Hey. I *knew* I could do this.

"Uh, no, we can do that," the editor said. Well, you can't blame a girl for trying. I glanced over at Mr. Emerson, who was shaking his head and smiling. "You have more guts than a burglar," he chuckled.

I shrugged and smiled. "Never hurts to ask," I said.

Later I caught up to Eddie at his locker. "Hey, Eddie," I called. "How would you like to say 'hot dog' again?"

23

It seemed like the whole school was excited and asking questions and tugging on me. I could hardly think straight. But all I really wanted was to get home, call the missionaries, and ask more questions.

Jimmy was back after being suspended, and was evidently unrepentant. He wasted no time in trying to pick up where he left off in his "Mission: Megan Pitney" scheme. He was standing by the door to the English class, grinning and trying to get my eye. But so many kids were crowding in to talk to me—about Courtney and Governor Barrett and the TV interview—that Jimmy couldn't get close enough to say anything. I could see his head popping into view between a bunch of kids, then I noticed he would try to circle around and squeeze in from another angle.

When class was ready to start, there was still a cluster of kids around my desk, and Cryson had to rap on her desk with a pointer to get them to scatter. Then she congratulated me for doing CPR, and said everyone was excited to hear about my upcoming interview with the governor.

During class, Jimmy kept trying (unsuccessfully) to whisper to me, and once leaned so far into the aisle that I almost laughed. At one point he passed me a note which said, "I need to talk to you about the classes at your Mom's studio." Finally the bell rang, and since Cryson wanted to see Jimmy after class, that left me free to zip out of the room without having to speak a word to him.

After school I called Mom to tell her about the TV interview, and she almost became boisterous. She dashed right home, leaving her assistant, Alicia, in charge of the studio. She ran to her closet to find "something chic—no, smart" to wear. For both of us. I just laughed. This woman will never change.

Mom coached me on keeping my chin down and speaking slowly for the camera, then left me alone to battle with my impossible hair. I tried parting it different ways, pinning it back, letting it alone, and finally decided to declare a moral victory and leave it at that.

When the reporters arrived, I was sitting there in one of Mom's "Donnas" (she speaks of Donna Karan as if they're old pals), looking—no doubt—like a fourteen-year-old kid playing dress-up in Mom's clothes. Mom was wearing a Gucci scarf ("blue is so smashing on camera"), an Armani jacket, and Christian Dior pantyhose.

"We look ridiculous," I said. I watched the crew from the window. They had cameras and lights and microphones, all connected to what seemed like an impossible tangle of cords and wires. "Look. Those guys are all in Levi's."

Mother joined me at the window to watch them unload their equipment. "Those fellows are all *behind* the scenes, Veronica. We're the *stars*."

I swallowed nervously. Then the doorbell rang and Mother opened it, her teeth a gleaming crescent. Self-conscious around someone so breathtakingly beautiful, the camera crew nevertheless managed to set up all their equipment. Then a field reporter, Mike Haines, sat me and Mother—how could he resist?—on the sofa. Mom was smiling like a movie queen; I was sweating like a bullet factory.

Mike looked into the camera. "I'm here with Veronica Halston, the young girl who will be flying to the state capitol soon to interview Governor Barrett. But an unusual turn of events made Veronica cancel the original interview to spend time with her friend. Veronica, exactly what happened?"

The lights were so bright! My fingers were trembling. I took a deep breath (Mom's advice) to ease the butterflies. "Well, my friend had a cardiac arrest, and I just felt I should stay with her."

"You performed CPR on her until paramedics arrived, isn't that right?"

"Yes." I glanced over at Mom. She was still grinning and mugging for the camera, not even listening. I could have said, "Well, my house burned down and my mother ran off with the circus and I became a belly dancer," and she would still have sat there beaming.

"And when you called the governor to cancel your interview, what did he say?"

"Well, I spoke to his secretary. But later, he wanted to fly me up to see him."

"What made you think of interviewing him in the first place?"

I thought about Uncle Scott and Aunt Mia, but a nudge from Mother—who must have been listening, after all—made me reconsider my answer. "Well, he *is* the governor," I said. "Who wouldn't want to interview him?"

"Yes, but you're only seventeen," Mike persisted. This guy was beginning to remind me of Aunt Mia. And of Jimmy Murdock, too, with his perfect looks and that same sappy grin.

Suddenly I felt a surge of confidence. "I consider myself a journalist," I said. "Like you. I wanted to interview Governor Barrett. I know I'm only a junior, but I can report, just the same as anyone else."

"Whoa—ho! Okay! Good for you!" Mike was understandably startled. "And what made you stay with your friend instead of reaching that goal?"

I just looked at him. Wasn't it obvious? "She's my *friend*," I said, leaving a big, unspoken "duh" hanging in the air. There was no other explanation.

Mike kept holding the microphone to my mouth as though I must surely have a better reason than that, but I just looked boldly back at him.

"Okay, cut," he said at last. "Veronica, thank you very much. Now, Ms. Halston, may we ask you a couple of questions, too?"

Cameras switched angles as Mother used her most buttery voice to say, "Surely." Ha. If he hadn't asked, she probably would have lassoed him with one of those lighting cords.

"Mrs. Halston," Mike said, "How does it feel to know your daughter saved her friend's life?"

"Very proud. You know, I run a modeling studio—"

(I could not believe she plugged her studio!)

Then she continued. "—so I live in a very narrow world. But Veronica has a broader view—she is truly dedicated to helping others, and doing good. This did not surprise me one bit."

My jaw dropped. "Mom," I found myself saying, ever so softly.

But she wasn't through. "Veronica is one of those 'bigger than life' characters you usually only read about. Can I tell you something? It's a little intimidating to be the mother of such a brilliant girl." Then she smiled. "I can't wait to watch her as she takes on the world."

I stared at her, dumbstruck, and Mike turned back to the camera. "Thanks to Veronica, Principal Gordon Emerson of Jefferson High School says he's going to make CPR mandatory training for every student in his school. This is Mike Haines, reporting."

The temperature dropped noticeably as they killed the lights. I was still staring at Mother, in such shock that I scarcely noticed the camera crew packing up and leaving. They were on their way to Courtney's next, as she had agreed to be interviewed also.

"Mom," I said, as the last of the crew members left, "I didn't know you felt that way about me."

She shrugged, and I think I noticed a little wetness in her eyes. I stood up. "Wait a second," I said, turning her to face me. "Do you mean that all this time you've been *proud* of me, and I have to hear it on *television* to find this out?"

We both laughed, and Mother hugged me. "Didn't you know before?"

I was still shaking my head in disbelief. "No; I always thought *you* were the bigger-than-life, intimidating one. I mean, you're so beautiful and you have this glamorous life, and I'm this short, frizzy-haired daughter. I . . . I've always thought you were ashamed of me."

Now Mother frowned, clearly stunned. "Veronica! How can you say that?"

"I just . . . that's how it's always seemed to me. You're always trying to fix the way I look and all. . . ."

Mother shook her head, then pulled me close. "I worry that you're embarrassed by *me*. My work is so . . . frivolous compared to the things you're interested in."

We smiled and stared at each other for a few minutes. My brain was receiving entirely too much new information lately. Just how much can one girl's brain absorb, anyway?

I began to cry. I couldn't even tell if I was happy or sad. I just needed a release. Mom held me as we both wiped our tears.

TWELFTH GRADER TREATED FOR SHOCK
Discovers Mother is Proud of Her

In a startling revelation this afternoon, Veronica Halston learned that Mitzi Halston, of the perfect cheekbones and ideal body type, actually feels intimidated by her relentlessly spunky daughter. Despite having inherited none of the attributes which have launched her mother's charmed life, Veronica discovered today that her mother actually admires her for herself. "I guess I have other valuable qualities," Veronica was found mumbling when she was admitted to the psychiatric ward. . . .

I whispered "I love you" into Mother's ear. She pulled away for a second and stared at me. Her face was streaked with tears, and she wasn't even blotting them away. Then she swept me into a hug so hard I thought I'd break. But I didn't care. I wanted this moment to last for the rest of my life.

24

That night on the news I saw Mother, who looked truly dazzling; myself, who looked not at all bad for a beginner; and Courtney, who, despite her illness, looked better than any of us. "Now *that's* photogenic," Mother observed.

"Honestly," Courtney was saying on the television, "if it hadn't been for Veronica, I would've died. I feel very grateful to be alive."

"What exactly brought on the cardiac arrest?" Mike asked.

"The main cause was anorexia nervosa," Courtney said. "I know a lot of girls who have this, so I appreciate the chance to speak out and warn them that it can honestly kill."

"You're all right now?"

"Well, I'm better than I was," Courtney said. She seemed a little weak, but the fire and fight was definitely there. "I still have to see a counselor and work to overcome this and get my health back. It's a long road. But I'm determined not to let this happen again."

"We wish you the best and appreciate your candor in speaking out," Mike said. Then the tape cut back to his question to me about Courtney when I said, "She's my friend."

I called Courtney to tell her how gorgeous she looked, and how proud I was of her for reaching out to help other girls. She said I should wear my mom's clothes more often because I looked so beautiful. "So," I said, "it's the clothes!"

As soon as we hung up, the phone started ringing. It seemed everyone we knew had been watching. Dad finally got through and said he was so proud that he'd popped a button on his shirt. I laughed. "Courtney really looked good, huh?"

"Yep. Courtney, your mother, and you looked sensational. You belong on there in Mike Haines' shoes."

"Oh, no. I think he wears an eleven, Dad."

And then the media floodgates opened. The next two weeks were a complete zoo. First, a woman from United Press International called and wanted to put the story on the national wire service. Then I got pulled out of class to talk to a man from National Public Radio. Five different newspaper reporters called. Three other radio stations interviewed me, as well as the editors of two magazines.

Jimmy Murdock finally found me in a hall and was tripping all over himself, trying to walk with me and be part of the deluge of well-wishers and curious kids asking about my upcoming trip. To be honest, the word "annoying" kept coming to mind.

Even Lauren, whose knees used to turn to jelly at the mere mention of his name, whispered, "This guy is *gross!*" into my ear. I laughed and spotted Eddie coming out of the computer room.

"Eddie," I shouted. "Hey, buddy!"

Jimmy's head looked like a spectator's at a ping-pong match. Back and forth he whipped, first looking at Eddie, then me, then back to Eddie, then back to me. It was hilarious. He couldn't believe I was chummy with Eddie the Geek. And he was furious that I was ignoring him and fawning over Eddie.

Eddie was fabulous. Watching all those old movies had taught him every Cary Grant move in the book. He stepped right between Jimmy and me and slapped Jimmy on the back. "How's it going, Jimmy?" Then before even waiting for an answer (a typical Murdock move, actually), he turned and gave my shoulders a squeeze. "Hi, baby, what's new?" (Another classic Murdock impersonation.) I hadn't realized what close attention Eddie had been paying to Jimmy's style. But he had the guy down pat.

I laughed so hard I dropped my math book, and both Eddie and Jimmy dived for it. I could definitely get used to this kind of treatment. Fortunately, Eddie got the book first and tucked it under his arm.

"What's this—chivalry?" I asked Eddie, clearly pleased. "I don't know many guys who carry girls' books for them these days." Then I gave Jimmy an obvious glance.

"Now you do," Eddie grinned. We turned a corner and Jimmy bumped smack into Coach Barnes, who immediately pulled him aside. Jimmy, who would love to get back onto the football team, was suddenly torn between sports and girls, and was trying to be polite to Coach Barnes while still pursuing me for a hook-up with Megan Pitney. Finally, Eddie and I slipped away.

After school, two of the newspaper reporters came by. Both of them also wanted to be at the airport when Governor Barrett flew me to the capitol. Evidently the governor's office had told everybody about what a great story of friendship this was, and two of the TV news stations were planning airport shots, too. It was weird; I'd always wanted to be the news reporter, but I never thought I'd be the news *maker*.

Then the City Press asked if I'd write an article about my visit with the governor! Me—printed in the local paper! One of the TV news stations called Courtney again, wanting to do a week-long special report on anorexia, beginning with her story.

In the midst of all this, Mom asked why I wasn't more excited about it. I stopped and thought. Because something even more exciting was happening? How do you tell someone that you think maybe you've stumbled onto Christ's true church, and that everything else pales by comparison?

"I think it's Courtney's church," I said. "I guess I'm preoccupied with that right now."

Mother stared at me like I was from Jupiter. What could be more exciting than fame? She was speechless.

I asked the missionaries to come over again, and Courtney joined them. This time Mom peeked in now and then, just to see what could possibly top the flurry of media attention that had suddenly fallen into my lap.

Elder Kinsey wore the biggest wing tips I've ever seen in my life. A sharp Adam's apple rose up and down above his white collar, and his eyes twinkled silvery blue. He reminded me of a scientist, somehow. I could picture him in a lab coat, mixing formulas and saying, "Eureka!" I guess it was his combination of intellect and enthusiasm.

Elder Tellman looked a lot like me. He was short, red-haired, and seemed to have a streak of spunk in there somewhere. He was spiritual, too, and often teared up and had to clear his throat before going on.

Everything they said sounded solid, and all of it was backed up with scriptures from both the Bible and modern-day scriptures. I even liked that there was more than just the Bible for reference. The news reporter in me liked the idea of a lot of witnesses and sources. (I think I was the youngest kid at my grade school to turn in a report with a bibliography.) After all, why would Christ only visit some of the people on earth? It seemed logical to me that he loved them all equally, and he would visit them all. And they would keep records. Who knows—maybe even more of these records will be discovered in future years. Maybe records from Asia or someplace. Maybe *I'll* get to tell the world about it from headlines in the *New York Times!*

There were a zillion other things I liked, too. For one thing, I liked that God and Jesus were separate beings, not a blend. Even as a little kid, I remember hearing people refer to God and Jesus as the same "person," and found it very confusing. Even with the limited information I had about Bible stories, I knew that Jesus had prayed—and who else could he pray to but someone separate from himself?

It all rang true. Baptism by immersion was how Jesus did it, and it's how Mormons do it. They used to build temples; Mormons still build temples. They used to have apostles; Mormons today have apostles.

I also liked how they have no paid clergy; everyone volunteers in addition to their regular careers. And they don't pass a collection plate. Members are supposed to tithe ten percent of their increase, but they do it in private envelopes instead of in front of everyone else. The tithing doesn't bother me. I figure if you earn money with abilities God gave you, that's the least you can give back. Besides, all churches have expenses, and if you're going there and getting something out of it, you shouldn't expect somebody else to pay for that.

Courtney mentioned Zack's baptism, and I was surprised that it had only happened recently. Why wasn't he baptized as a baby? The elders explained that before age eight, you're really not accountable and can't technically "sin." I thought about this. It was absolutely right. "Then babies who die aren't condemned?"

"Oh, no," Courtney said. "They go to heaven. And their parents finish raising them once they're together again."

What a concept! I'd never known anybody who lost a baby, but it isn't hard to imagine the agony you'd feel. I would feel tremendous comfort if that happened to me, knowing that someday I would be able to finish raising my child.

"Boy, this is excellent," I whispered. "Who thought of all these great ideas?"

The elders laughed, thinking I was making a joke. And then I remembered: Oh, yeah. This is *Christ's* church. Well, no wonder.

They even believed that you have to do more than just say you're sorry when you repent. You have to change your heart and actions. That made sense to me. And Christ's suffering was to pay the price for all of our mistakes, so we can go back into the presence of God someday. Christ literally paid the price. And all we have to do (but we *do* have to do it) is repent. Justice and mercy combined. This was phenomenal. No mysteries, nothing unexplainable. No matter what points I challenged, they had the answers.

Mom stepped in and sat down just as they were describing the commitment a person makes when they join. "This isn't a church you just attend on Christmas and Easter," one of the elders said. He himself was a convert, and used to belong to a church like that. "A minister preached each week, a paid choir sang, and we just went and sat," he said. "But in this church, adults are given jobs to do. You need to be prepared to be fully involved. You could be asked to speak from the pulpit, teach classes, head up committees, run organizations . . ."

I glanced at Mom, the original Take Charge Woman, who was smiling. "So your women are very involved? I had thought Mormon women weren't allowed to do much."

Courtney laughed, then covered her mouth. "Oh, Mrs. Halston," she said. "They're exhausted."

Elder Kinsey smiled. "There are more leadership opportunities for women in this church than in any church I've seen. No, they don't hold the priesthood. But, along with everyone in the world, they benefit directly from it—the same as men do."

Elder Tellman said, "It can definitely keep you busy."

"I guess we're bracing you for full involvement," Elder Kinsey laughed. "It's not a church people join and then flake out on."

"Oh, please," Courtney said. "Veronica has never flaked out on anything in her life."

Then he explained about home teachers and visiting teachers. I liked this idea. It seems a church should make regular contact with its members. It sounded like the kind of ministry Jesus set up.

"Do the members pick the pastors?" Mother asked.

"No," Elder Tellman said. "The Lord does. They're called bishops, and they're chosen through revelation."

"But what if a bishop doesn't interpret the Bible the same way some of his parishioners do?" Mother asked. I was pleased that she seemed curious.

"There's really not much quarreling over scripture," Elder Kinsey said. "We rely on our prophet to interpret scripture, and it will match in every congregation. You can't go from a ward in Florida to a ward in Oregon and see doctrinal differences. Truth is truth, and it isn't really up to individual speculation."

I liked this! Jesus didn't say, "Well, here's my opinion—take it and see what you can do with it."

"Imagine," said Elder Tellman, "if everyone just made up their own brand of Christianity. You'd have chaos and confusion—little factions fighting and splitting off. In fact, that's what happened in the early history of the church, after the apostles were killed."

Mother smiled. "You really believe your prophet speaks for God?"

The elders nodded. "That's why we can trust in what he tells us to be true."

The phone rang then, and Mother excused herself to answer it.

"You know," I said to Courtney and the elders, "I was going to start my own church someday, with a lot of these same things in it."

Courtney smiled. "Why does this not surprise me?" Then she turned to the elders. "Veronica wants to redesign cars to put the engines on top. And she'll probably do it."

I laughed. "Hey—they should be at eye level so it'd be easier to work on them. Not where somebody can crash into them and make them blow up. And the way they are now, for every little repair you have to crawl under them on dollies, or lift the thing up with hydraulics. I mean, you talk about an idea that was *not* inspired—"

"Uh, back to the discussion," Elder Kinsey winked. "So you were going to design a church, too?"

"Well, not if you've already got one with all my ideas in it," I said. "And if it's already set up . . . and by *Christ*, no less . . ." I grinned at the elders and they chuckled, still unsure about when I was joking and when I was serious. "I mean, the priesthood. That I could not have invented."

"True," Elder Kinsey smiled. "That would be a tough one."

"So, maybe it's time for me to attend and see just how weird all you Mormons really are." The elders stared. "I was kidding," I said. They sighed with relief.

"We knew that," Elder Tellman said.

25

Of course, I'd been to a few youth nights with Courtney, but this would be my first glimpse of an actual service. I was with my dad that weekend, and he said he'd be happy to let Courtney's family pick me up to attend church with them.

All week I studied their literature and read the Book of Mormon. Between that, homework, and the media interviews about Courtney, I was swamped.

"Hey, Mom," I asked Friday night as I was waiting for Dad to pick me up. "How come you don't mind it that I'm looking into the Mormon church?"

"Why should I mind it?" she said. "They're good people, at least the ones I know. Besides, I know you wouldn't join anything you didn't check out completely," and she rolled her eyes to emphasize the word "completely."

I smiled, choosing to take her exaggeration as a compliment. And it did feel good to know that she trusted my judgment. "True," I winked. "So, what about you? Are you interested?"

She smiled. "I don't think so. Do you wish I was?"

I thought. "I might, if I really go through with this. I mean, don't you think it's exciting that Christ's original church could have been restored?"

She sighed. "I admire you. You've always been a deeper thinker than I am. I just never gave religion a whole lot of thought." She shrugged. "Maybe I should."

Dad drove up, and I wondered how he would react. He knew I was going to church with Courtney, but I hadn't really told him how serious my interest was. Naturally, I hit him with it the minute I got in the car. "Hey, guess what? I might be joining the Mormon church," I said.

Dad almost hit a steel post. He swerved over to the side of the road and threw the car into park. "You *what?*"

"I'm thinking about joining Courtney's church. I've been learning about it, and it's pretty cool."

Dad was forcing his eyes to blink. "Give a guy some warning, will you? I don't even get a 'Hi, how ya doin', Dad?'"

I laughed. "Hi, how ya doin', Dad? I'm thinking of joining the Mormon church. How's that?"

He gave a grand sigh and leaned back in his seat, his eyes closed. I wasn't sure how he was going to react to this information, but it felt good and strong and right as I'd said it.

Finally he looked over at me and smiled. Then he pulled back onto the road. "Since you're not asking my permission," he said, "as if you ever have—"

"Okay, okay," I interrupted. "*May* I join that church? Sheesh!"

"Yes." That was it. He said yes.

I grinned, dying of curiosity. "How come?"

Now Dad was sputtering, completely perplexed. "Aren't you glad I said yes? I have to defend the answer you wanted? What is this? Whose kid are you, really? Why do you challenge a yes answer?"

Now I was laughing. "I'm not challenging it," I said. "I'd just like to know why you said yes."

Suddenly Dad looked smug. "Well, I'm not going to tell you."

"What?! You *have* to! You can't just give a person a yes answer and not have a reason!"

"I do have a reason. I'm just not telling you what it is."

"DAD!" I couldn't believe he was doing this. "Tell me!"

Now he grinned. "Nope. For once I have you in suspense. Little Miss Curiosity, cornered at last. Dying to know something, and she can't find it out. Wheee!"

Now I began pummeling his shoulder with my fists, laughing and growling at the same time. "This should be illegal!" I shouted. Dad was in his glory, laughing and holding this piece of information over me.

"Fine," I said, folding my arms. "Don't tell me."

"Okay, I won't."

"DAD!" This man was definitely too much like me.

That Sunday, I went to church with the Calhouns. It was not what I had expected. It didn't seem eery and quiet like the echoing cathedrals I've visited on vacations. In fact, you could hear a lot of babies crying. "Sorry it's so noisy," Courtney whispered. I shrugged. Actually, the noise didn't bother me. It felt like being at a big family reunion—warm and cozy. A whole family was giving the talks that day, and I liked how even the five-year-old could give one. He talked about Noah's Zark!

After the first meeting, Courtney said we'd be going to two youth classes. As we walked through the bustling hall, she said, "Veronica, I really haven't been a very good missionary. I . . . I don't know why you're even looking into the Church after the bad example I set."

I stared at her. "What are you talking about?"

"My eating disorder and all—not to mention a million other weaknesses I have—"

"Oh, come off it," I said, trying to pull her out of the pool of self-pity she was creating. "So you have to be perfect to show someone Christ's church? How could *anybody* ever do it, if they wait until they're perfect to speak up?"

She smiled. "I guess."

"You guess? You know I'm right. You have a problem, okay. You're working on it. We all have problems, Courtney. The fact that you're working on it says a lot. And you've been a great example. I can't even think how many times you've talked to me about . . . what is it you're always saying? Values."

Just then we turned into a classroom, and there on the wall was a poster about the very values Courtney had been talking about!

"Ah. . ." I said, scanning the list. "And all this time I thought you came up with those yourself. You are such a disappointment."

Now we both laughed, and Courtney squeezed my hand.

Some other kids came in and sat down, then class started. The teacher asked Courtney to introduce me. She stood up. "This is my friend, Veronica Halston," she said. "She's an investigator."

"Psst!" I hissed. "I'm an investigative reporter, not a detective."

Courtney looked at the floor, her shoulders shaking as she tried not to laugh.

The teacher said, "It looks like your guest can speak for herself."

Naturally, I popped right up. "I'm not an investigator," I said, "I'm someone who's looking into your church."

The teacher, whom everyone called Sister Salisbury, smiled. "In our church, 'investigator' means exactly that."

"Oh," I said. "Darn. I was hoping to be called a looker."

They got the joke and laughed! Well, this was refreshing.

The whole morning went great. The two classes were about serving others and setting goals. There was a lot of stimulating discussion, and I was impressed by how well the others knew the Bible and the Book of Mormon. "You guys are intimidating," I said.

"Oh, you'll pick it right up," one of the other girls said. And I believed her. Again, I felt as if a wonderful hug was closing in.

After church, I told the missionaries I was ready to be baptized. This felt right, and I knew the feelings were coming from the Holy Ghost, not from myself. Courtney encircled me with her thin arms and held me tight. We cried.

In the next few days Courtney made great progress, and she came back to school looking as strong as ever. She was nervous about being teased, but everyone was super supportive. Especially the teachers. They made her out to be quite a heroine, and I was greatly relieved. Her homeroom even gave her flowers.

At first when all the fuss over us began, it made me uncomfortable. Here was a near-tragedy, and it felt like a media circus. I felt uneasy in the "hero" role, because I knew I had only done what anybody else would have. I also worried about Courtney losing her privacy. But she handled it perfectly, and used the attention to launch a positive crusade, publicizing the dangers of anorexia and the importance of knowing CPR.

She even began rehearsing for Mom's fashion show, and was as excited as ever for her big debut.

In some ways, all this attention has helped me to understand Mother better. I know what it feels like, now, to stand out from the crowd, to be noticed and special. On the one hand, the attention feels great—there's the ego-gratification of all those fans. On the other hand, there's a sense that you can't just let your hair down and be a regular person; you have a "public" and they have expectations. You have to get used to being stared at. I wondered if celebrities feel this bittersweet reaction to fame. I can see where it could twist your priorities if you're not careful. You could start believing that all your "admirers" really like you for your inside self—and probably they're only smitten by your image, or by something you've done, like winning a ball game. You could even start to believe you're as perfect as the papers say—which, of course, nobody is.

It hit me that this is how Mom's entire life has felt. She's been trying to balance her career with being a single mom, and on top of everything else, being a high-profile person who never has the luxury of a bad hair day.

How does anybody navigate such a twisting river without that Values poster I saw at Courtney's church? Faith, Divine Nature, Individual Worth, Knowledge, Choice and Accountability, Good Works, and Integrity. It's like a map! Those are the keys to keeping your feet on the ground, even when fame falls in your lap.

26

February second came roaring up the road in the form of a black limousine, ready to take me to the airport.

Dad had sent me a beautiful bouquet of roses with the card, "Knock 'em dead, Ronnie" attached.

Eddie called just as the doorbell rang, and when I picked up the phone he said, "Happy Groundhog Day!"

I laughed. "Eddie, go soak."

"I just thought I'd call you on this important occasion. I mean, it *is* a national holiday. Nothing else very important is happening today, is it?"

"Eddie, they're here to pick me up right now! I can't talk."

"Oh—sorry! Hey, good luck. No fooling. You are going to be awesome."

Eddie, you *are awesome*. "Thanks, Eddie. I'll call you when I get back."

Then I got into the car with Mother. I stretched my feet all the way out in front of me and took in my surroundings: a telephone, walnut paneling, indirect lighting, plush velour seats, a TV, a plexiglass divider between the front and back seats. "I think I could handle this on a regular basis," I said.

Mother was beaming, which struck me as unusual. She usually takes ritzy things in stride. But she was really smiling.

"Hey, how are you going to get back to the studio if you see me off at the airport?" I asked.

"Oh—he'll drive me," she said, nodding at the chauffeur.

I looked out at the other cars on the freeway, waiting for

someone to look in to see what famous person was in my limo. Finally a truck driver peered in, and I waved. I glanced back at Mother, but she didn't say a word.

At the airport I had brief interviews with the TV and newspaper reporters who had asked to cover my departure. Travelers with suitcases and garment bags gathered behind me, trying to get a peek at the commotion. Then my flight was announced, and Mother walked me to the gate.

"Well, good luck on the fashion show. I'm sure it will be wonderful, and I'm sorry I can't be there. Please have somebody take a lot of pictures," I said. "I'm sure it will be fine."

"Yes," Mother said, "Alicia will do a wonderful job as emcee."

I looked at her, puzzled. "Alicia? How come you're not doing it?"

"I've asked her to fill in for me while we fly up to the capitol," Mother said.

"What?" I couldn't believe my ears.

"Come, Veronica, they're boarding." I gasped and blinked the whole way as Mother led me by the arm.

"What—how?" My whole body felt like it was smiling.

"I bought myself a ticket," she said, still grinning that limousine grin. Then in a sweeping flourish, she pulled it from her handbag and waved it like a feather boa.

I stumbled to the airplane and found my seat. "What about your fashion show?"

"I want you to know that I love you, Veronica." Mother slid her purse under the seat in front of her.

I gulped. Was this really Mitzi? *My* Mitzi? "You don't have to prove anything to me," I said.

"I know I don't have to. I *want* to. When you're eighty-five years old, I want you to remember that when you were seventeen and interviewed the governor—for the *first* time"—and then she winked, "your mother was right there beside you."

I was never so happy. Never. I hugged her and cried onto her shoulder. *We can actually be friends*, I thought. It felt glorious. I wanted to bask in that shimmering, loving moment forever. Yes, I *did* want her to join the Church. I wanted this feeling for eternity. And all at once I knew that neither a governor, nor anyone else, could ever possibly top it.

27

When we landed, some men were standing inside the terminal holding a sign that said "Halston." I saw them before Mom did, and darted over.

"Hey, that's no Halston—that's Yves Saint Laurent!" I hollered, eyeballing one of the guy's suits. I turned to look at Mom, sure she would be laughing at her clever daughter.

She looked mortified.

The two men were glancing at each other, not sure whether to smile or not.

"Hi! I'm Veronica Halston," I said, sticking out my hand to shake theirs. I'd never felt bolder.

The man in horn-rimmed glasses pushed them up onto his nose, as if to get a better look at this brazen kid. The other, a gorgeous hunk of an aide and the one wearing the Yves Saint Laurent suit, smiled a broad, toothy grin. "I'm Grant Oliver, and this is Carlisle Rose. We're from Governor Barrett's office."

"I was just kidding," I said, more for Mother's benefit than for theirs. Hey, I wanted to say to her, *you're* the one who taught me all about fashion designers and clothes and stuff. She had now inched feebly over to join us, embarrassment in her eyes. Darn. Just when everything had been going so well.

"I'm Mitzi Halston," she said, extending her delicate hand like a flower. "I thought I'd surprise Veronica and join her on this special trip. She is very honored."

Uh-oh. Here we go again, talking in my behalf. Only this time I felt tingly and brave, proud as Dad with his popped buttons. Today

I was going to speak for myself, come Mitzi or high water.

"That's right," I chimed in. "I really appreciate Governor Barrett's flying me up here. I'm looking forward to meeting him."

"Good. He feels the same way," Mr. Oliver said. He walked us outside. "We've heard a lot about you, Veronica. How is your friend doing?"

"She's doing great. She's been on the news warning other girls about anorexia, and I'm sure she'll get stronger and stronger."

Mr. Rose pushed his glasses up again. "We'll be talking with members of the press later on. I'll brief you as we drive to the capitol."

"How do you like that?" I whispered to Mother. "He's going to *brief* me!" I felt so important I couldn't believe it. Me, visiting the governor; me, riding in a limousine; me, being "briefed as we drive to the capitol."

Another limo, just like the last one, screeched up to the sidewalk. "Wow! That guy drives *fast*," I said to Mother, trying to make another joke. Mr. Oliver and Mr. Rose stared at me as the driver opened the door. Mother smiled and sighed before slipping into the back seat. I knew she was thinking, *Veronica, don't be boisterous.* But I had to hand it to her; she was really controlling those corrective impulses in front of government officials.

Then just as I was about to get into the car after her, I turned to Mr. Oliver. "Hey—wait a minute. How do I know you're really from the governor's office? I mean, you could be kidnappers or terrorists or anything."

An audible Mitzi Gasp floated out of the car.

Mr. Oliver laughed. "Right you are." He then produced his identification with a flourish even Mom would envy.

I smiled. "I just had to check."

I got into the back seat and Mom dug her claws into my arm. "What are you *doing?*" she hissed.

"Mom, give me a break," I whispered back. "I saw that on television, and it is totally possible."

Her frozen goddess profile was silhouetted against the light of the bright window as we pulled away from the curb. It was hard to unwind when I felt this excited, but I took a deep breath and tried. I knew I'd better tone down and relax, or this time I'd be canceling the governor's interview to visit my *mother* in the hospital.

GIRL GIVES MOTHER A STROKE
Doctors Warn Kids Not to Embarrass Parents

A limousine became an ambulance today when Mitzi Halston of the Mitzi Halston Modeling School suffered a stroke en route to Governor Barrett's office. Her 17-year-old daughter, Veronica, is being held without bond.

"I was just jumpy," Veronica said, an excuse prosecutors say will not hold much weight in court.

"This woman nearly died," said Dr. Frank Martin, the neuro-surgeon on the case. "These kids today don't realize how humiliating they can be."

Just as we pulled into the circular drive at the steps of the capitol, Mom whispered, "Now might be the proper time to exercise some restraint, be a little reserved, humble—"

I grinned and leaped eagerly onto the curb. Mother sighed.

Mr. Rose told me to just relax and enjoy talking with a reporter from *Time Magazine*, another from *USA Today*, and the local network news crews. I just knew Mom was aching to add, "Relax? That's the problem! She's *too* relaxed."

"Just be yourself," Mr. Rose said. Mom cringed.

The capitol rotunda was massive. There were huge marble pillars, gleaming bright banisters, even a marble mosaic of the state seal inlaid in the floor. I remember looking at the colorful parquetry on the floor and thinking, *What a great floor for a kid to play on—and there probably isn't a kid for miles around.*

Our voices echoed up to the domed ceiling, around the sparkling chandeliers, and back down to us again. The men led us to some elevators. All was quiet as we stepped inside and watched the tiny gold lights blink on and off as we rode up, up, up into Pure Panic.

Suddenly I realized that was what I was feeling. This wasn't confidence—this was the height of hysteria masked by a babbling mouth. The elevator stopped, and I felt paralyzed with fright. *We're actually at the governor's office,* I thought. *He's within a few yards of me.* I wanted to die.

Mother was behind me, pushing me out of the elevator and hissing, "Veronica, pick up your feet!" I felt the color draining from my face. Suddenly I wanted to go home, burrow into bed, and stay there for the rest of my life.

Mom kept pushing me in the small of my back, like a hold-up man with a pistol. My stiff legs skidded out in front of me.

Mr. Rose was holding open the elevator doors, which kept trying to close, and Mr. Oliver, who had stepped out in front to lead the way, was now peering curiously back and no doubt wondering what the delay was.

Finally I gave in and walked, my knees shaking. There was a drinking fountain in the hall, and Mother motioned to it. "Oh, yes," I almost shouted. "I really need a drink!" Mr. Rose's glasses nearly fell off his head. Mother emitted a little anguished groan at my remark, and I gulped the icy water.

"She meant water, of course," Mother was saying when I came up for air. Mr. Rose was still looking at me with those magnified, puzzled eyes behind his horn-rims.

Mr. Oliver was standing beside me, grinning again. "Feeling a little nervous?"

I smiled and nodded. "I'm only seventeen," I said, sounding like I was pleading my case before a jury on charges of First Degree Lunacy.

Mr. Oliver smiled. What a gorgeous guy. I felt light-headed and silly. "But I'm mature for my age," I added. Then, realizing how ridiculous that sounded (and noting that Mother was rolling her eyes), I said with a bit of self-deprecating sarcasm, "I guess you noticed that."

Then Mr. Oliver laughed, and even Mr. Rose smiled. "You'll do just fine," Mr. Oliver said.

I sighed. The terror was gone, and all that was left was a lump of nervousness I could deal with. We pushed through double doors into a reception room. There sat a woman at a desk with a sign reading, "Janice Montease."

"It's a pleasure finally meeting you," I said, extending my hand.

"This is my mother, Mitzi Halston."

Mom smiled, and her edginess evaporated. "How do you do." Her voice was like cool, sweet liquid. Mother looked gorgeous. I was really proud to have her there, since everyone always treats her like royalty, and the way I was blabbering and bungling so far, it was nice to have someone nearby who knew what to say and how to behave. That way, in case they were all wondering what on earth they had gotten into, they could always glance over at Mom and think, Well, at least her mother seems normal.

Mrs. Montease was older than she sounded on the phone, but also prettier. Her handsome gray hair was cut in the latest style, and the word that came to mind when I looked at her suit was "crisp." Her mannerisms were as smooth and flawless as Mother's. She smiled and seemed genuinely happy we were there, and suddenly I felt like Little Orphan Annie visiting Daddy Warbucks.

Mrs. Montease came around her desk and put an arm around me. "I had no idea you were so pretty," she said.

And guess what—I didn't scowl or laugh or smirk. I just said, "Thank you." Mother beamed.

You know, I really did look pretty good. I mean, for me. Mom had dressed me from head to toe so I wouldn't have to worry about my clothes, and I looked exactly right for the occasion. I was wearing blue DKNY ("Advertising research has shown that men react favorably to blue," Mom said), and my hair was tamed by three gallons of Mom's gel. ("Simplicity is elegance," Mother had said. "This makes the right statement: You're young but you're sharp. You don't want to look silly or frilly; this is the time for sophistication. Yet, you want to look your age.") In short, I looked great.

I wondered what the governor would be wearing. He probably got up and sleepily climbed into one of his regular work suits. Probably navy. Maybe gray. Probably didn't even think about it as he flung a tie around his neck and tied it in a fast Windsor. Slipped his feet into some shoes and thought momentarily of shining them, then said, "Oh, what for? She's just a kid," then grabbed a piece of toast, kissed his wife—who was in curlers, maybe—and came to work. Just another routine day.

Mrs. Montease asked us to wait a moment while she disappeared down another hallway. Soon she returned and led us to Governor Barrett's office. I took a deep breath.

28

"Hello! I'm Jack Barrett!" he bellowed as he came around his desk. "So you're Veronica."

I repeated the line I had memorized for this moment. "How do you do, Governor. This is my mother, Mitzi Halston."

"A pleasure, a pleasure," he said, clasping Mother's hand in both of his. He was brimming with enthusiasm and gusto. You'd have thought this was the campaign trail and we were big investors.

"Won't you sit down?" Governor Barrett's office was filled with gorgeous Victorian furniture, yet there didn't seem to be any place where you could sit down comfortably. Everything looked so delicate and breakable. Actually, Mom looked like the perfect porcelain doll to perch on one of the chairs, but she said, "I believe I'll just wait outside, thank you. Veronica can handle this on her own, can't you, darling?"

I grinned at her. "Thanks, Mom."

The governor looked exactly like his pictures, only in color. It was funny; I'd seen his photo in the newspapers and I hadn't expected to see a deeply tanned, blue-eyed man. Yet there he was, about twenty pounds overweight, a little blustery but jolly and energetic, his graying hair trimmed neatly and his tie knotted firmly in a double Windsor. I glanced down at his feet for a second; his shoes were shined after all. And he wore a tan wool suit, a white shirt, and a turquoise tie. Maybe this morning his wife had said to him, "Jack, you want to wear that tan suit with the turquoise tie. It's winter, it's conservative, but it's not stuffy. It makes the statement, 'I'm old but I'm sharp.' And be sure to shine your shoes."

"It's an honor to have you here at the capitol," Governor Barrett said. "I was very impressed with your decision to stay with your friend when she was hospitalized. You demonstrated great loyalty. And I understand you did the CPR that saved her."

"I really can't take all the credit," I said. "The paramedics came very fast, the hospital was great, and Courtney herself has a lot of fighting spirit. It all worked together. But thank you. I'm very honored to be here, and I appreciate your flying me all the way up here."

He smiled. He looked like he'd be a neat grandpa.

I paused and then went on. "You have a beautiful capitol."

"It's your capitol too, you know."

I grinned and looked around at his sumptuous office, the huge flags behind his French desk. "Yes, I guess you're right. It is, isn't it? I mean, once I begin paying taxes."

Now it was his turn to smile. "You looking forward to that, Veronica?"

I laughed. "When you're seventeen, *any* income seems like a lot. Even if you do have to give so much of it to the government." Oh—what was I saying? What a motor-mouth. I couldn't believe I had been with him just two minutes, and already I was complaining about taxes. I tried to back-pedal. "I mean, I guess you need them to run things. It's not that they're all bad."

Now he laughed. "How would you like to explain that to the voters in the next election? Seems most people think the government just runs on the wishes of the public."

And then we started rolling. I asked him if I could get right into the interview, and he seemed as eager as I was. I asked him about the committees to investigate committees to investigate nonexistent charities. I asked him about government spending on unnecessary airport expansion while there were cutbacks in education. I asked him who really backed various bills, and what they stood to gain by those bills passing. It was fantastic! He really became animated, and gave me answers that made me feel like he genuinely respected me. I used some of Mrs. Dregman's statistics and asked him about the new judges he would be appointing soon. I even knew about the weak records of a couple of them, and the governor raised his eyebrows.

"They teach you this in *high* school?"

I smiled and looked down at my notes. "No, they teach us to read in grade school. The rest I got from newspapers and stuff."

He smiled. I could tell I had surprised him. I'd made him a little uncomfortable, but he *liked* me. I could feel it. I'll bet when he was my age, the principal called his mother to ask that he be reined in, too.

"So are you going to support Rasmussen, even though he's soft on crime?"

The governor pointed a finger at me. "Begging the question." It was as though we were sparring in a friendly debate and trying to trip each other up.

"Okay, if he's not soft on crime," I said, discovering that a soft voice worked best with hard questions, "how do you explain his letting Freedman off in such a clear-cut murder case—when the defendant had actually signed a confession?"

Barrett buzzed an intercom machine on his desk. "Janice, get me the Freedman vs. Colton file, will you?"

This was really getting good. Mrs. Montease came in with a manila folder, and Barrett motioned me over to his desk. I leaned over and we looked at the record. He explained some things to me about plea bargaining, and I told him I thought plea bargaining was the sellout of the century.

And he laughed! Then he'd come up with some other point and I'd say, "Maybe so, but what about this—" around and around. I almost forgot to take notes. It was heaven.

Finally we got around to agriculture, and even weather. This somehow led us to take a break from the heavier issues, and I asked him if he always wore wool suits. He seemed a little flustered.

"Much of the time. But I wear short-sleeved shirts."

"Where do you shop?" I knew it wasn't a real reporter's question, but I was curious. Mitzi had raised me to wonder about these things.

"Ah. At last, a question I can answer without a sheaf of statistics to prove my point! I have them made for me, actually. I get a better fit, and I even save money."

"Really? Who makes them for you?"

"I have a wonderful Chinese tailor in Hong Kong. He doesn't speak a word of English, but he's a whiz with a pair of scissors."

"And you fly to Hong Kong to have the suits made?"

Governor Barrett's jovial countenance faded for a second, like a TV tube threatening to burn out momentarily. Then he smiled again, as if Hong Kong was just around the corner.

"On occasion." Barrett issued a manufactured chuckle.

I grinned. I had actually hit upon some kind of jackpot. This was a *story*. One of Barrett's big slogans was "Buy American," and here I'd caught him with his hands in the Fortune Cookie Jar.

GOVERNOR BARRETT EMPLOYS CHEAP FOREIGN LABOR
Costs Americans Jobs

"But aren't you quoted as saying we should support American-made products?" I asked.

He sighed. "You know what I'm glad about?"

I looked at him, kind of an impish grin on my face. "What?"

"I'm glad that by the time you'll really be dangerous, I'll be out of office."

I laughed. "Both could be sooner than you think," I said.

He shook his head, chuckling. "Okay, you win. I honestly hadn't thought of it that way, but I guess you're right, and I thank you for pointing this out. I will not have them make any more suits for me. Okay?"

I felt sheepish and looked down at my notes. He had flown me up here for this interview, and now I was cornering him. No wonder reporters don't like to accept gifts.

"You realize, of course, that the next time you see me I'll probably look tattered and torn," he teased. "With baggy pants and sagging shoulders."

I laughed, then said, "I didn't plan to be a problem."

He smiled good-naturedly. "The heck you didn't." And then we both laughed. "Come on," he said, rising from his chair. "Let's go meet the press—your colleagues."

"Oh, by the way," I said, "who did your office? I mean it's beautiful and everything, but it doesn't look like you." And it didn't. It was fussy and feminine, in fact.

"*Not* China," Barrett said. Then he looked at it with exasperation and muttered, "My wife."

Exactly as I had thought. I smiled at him. "She has exquisite taste, though." He shrugged and we grinned at each other. It was funny; I felt as if I knew a part of him his own wife didn't know.

"It needs heavier furniture and a . . . what? A bolder feeling, doesn't it?" he asked as we walked down the hall.

I smiled and nodded. "It should express your personality. Maybe some dark red leather wingbacks, a walnut desk, a bronze on the shelf behind you . . ."

Barrett's eyes nearly popped out of his head. "That is *exactly* what I wanted in the first place!" Then he did a deliberate double take at me and smiled. "You are one scary kid."

I laughed, and we rounded the corner to the reception room. Mother was sitting on the sofa looking ravishing. Mr. Rose and Mr. Oliver were sitting in nearby chairs, obviously unaware that they were both staring at her, and probably had been transfixed in this state for an hour.

"Janice, call Beth and tell her that Veronica here is going to redecorate Versailles for me."

I laughed again, and glanced at Mother. She was glowing with pride. I had asked the governor some really critical questions about controversial subjects, and even discovered a little hypocrisy. But what would please Mom would be to know that I had correctly evaluated his decor problem.

We headed down to the rotunda for a press conference. I was starting to feel comfortable with the governor, but now I got all nervous again. Nationwide coverage!

The reporters were surprisingly polite. Or possibly bowled over by Mother's beauty. Whatever it was, they were so considerate that the governor even joked, "Maybe I'll bring Veronica to all our press conferences; she seems to bring out the best in all of you."

They asked about Courtney, of course, and about learning CPR at school. I explained about Mr. Emerson's plan to make CPR mandatory training, and everybody was very impressed.

They asked how I had gotten the idea to interview the governor, and this time I didn't mind somebody else answering the question for me. "I'll tell you where she got it," Barrett said, his eyes twinkling. "She was *born* with it. This little lady is one tough reporter, so all of you had better watch out for your jobs. She really had me sweating a couple of times."

Just wait until I tell them about Hong Kong, I thought. Then I wondered what to do. I mean, I was his guest! On the other hand, if I glossed over it, that would be like selling out and writing an essay on deer hunting. I'll never make it as a journalist if I can be bought, right?

While the reporters were still chuckling at Barrett's joke, I glanced at Mom. She was standing in the background, looking absolutely proud and thrilled for me. She wasn't trying to upstage me this time, or plug her studio or speak in my behalf. It was as if I had come out of the governor's office a new person . . . and she had become one, too. I winked at her.

"I'd like you all to meet my mother," I said. "She missed a very important fashion show to fly up here with me."

Mom was blushing and waving away the attention now. "I wouldn't have missed this for anything," she murmured. I could tell her perfume was melting a young reporter nearby, whose microphone—aimed at Mother's Rapture Red lipstick—was nearly slipping from his fingers as he stared at her in wondering awe.

I thought about how wonderful it had felt on the airplane, and what a great surprise it was for her to support me like this. I felt like a princess again.

"She's a marvelous journalist," Mother said. "Very professional." The cluster of reporters looked back at me, not one of them sneering. They had respect for me. Better still, *Mom* had respect for me.

"What are you going to write about when you get home, Veronica?" someone shouted.

"You'll have to read the article," I said. "I will give you one bit of news, though."

Everything became as stone-still as the marble pillars around us. I looked up at the governor. He seemed like such a nice man, and I didn't want to get him into trouble. But still, I wanted him to stick to his word. "You'll be pleased to know that Governor Barrett had a call from Hong Kong while I was visiting with him. He had a chance to have his suits made over there for less money than they would cost him here."

Barrett stiffened.

"But," I said, "he turned it down because he really does believe in buying American products, just like he says. Right, Governor?"

He smiled the most grateful grin I've ever seen. "That's right," he said.

Another journalist shouted over the crowd, "Would you call this a once-in-a-lifetime experience, Veronica?"

I smiled into the cameras. "Not for me . . . I'll be back."

They all clapped and cheered.

"I'm sure you will," Barrett whispered in my ear. "I'm sure you will."

29

I typed up my stories as soon as I got home, one for the City Press and one for the school paper. That night I was all over the evening news. The next morning a neighborhood newspaper slapped down on our porch bearing the headline, "Local Girl Makes Mark."

"Oh, yuck," I said. "It makes me sound like a dog that isn't housebroken." But the article itself was okay, and I clipped it out to save in my growing scrapbook.

Then Dad called. "How's the celebrity this morning?"

"Back to the real world, basically."

Dad chuckled. "Yeah. That's how fame is, I think. At least, it's always been that way with me."

"Ha ha. Guess what?" Then I told him what really happened with the Hong Kong suits. He agreed with Mother that I had done the right thing. "You got the same result without embarrassing him," Dad said. "Everyone will be watching his clothes now, and he'll have no choice but to buy American."

"And I think I kept a friend," I said.

"So was it as exciting as you had hoped?"

"In a way," I said. "But nothing compared to this Saturday."

"Why—what's this Saturday?"

"My baptism. I've decided to join the Mormon church. Will you come?"

Dad was silent for a few seconds. "Absolutely. You sure about this?"

"Two hundred percent."

"Well, no doubt you have turned over every stone in your

research. . . ."

I laughed. "Actually, I thought that was how I'd decide—you know, analyze it to death. But the missionaries said I should wait for an answer to my prayers, not just base the decision on logic alone."

"So did you pray?" Dad and I had never talked about this before.

"Yeah. I did. And I got the feeling that I needed to be more patient, so I just kept on praying and waiting. And then, like in small steps, I felt better and better, until I just *knew* this is what I have to do."

"No sudden, dramatic answer?"

"Nope," I said. "Just a quiet feeling of being certain. Really certain."

"That's great," Dad said, almost in a whisper of respect. "I'll be there."

On Saturday, Mom asked what I was planning to wear, and I told her I would be baptized all in white.

"Oh, no, honey," she said. "You're an autumn. You should wear *off*-white."

I busted up laughing. "Good one, Mom. Everybody has to wear white when they're baptized."

"Oh." And she actually blushed. "Of course."

We met the elders at the church, and it seemed as if the whole youth organization was there to support me. Someone was playing the most beautiful piano music I'd ever heard. I looked over and it was Eddie!

"What are you doing here?" I whispered, a little embarrassed that I hadn't thought to invite him.

"Courtney told me about it, and I asked if I could come."

"I didn't know you could play like this."

"Well," he said, raising his eyebrows, "I'm a man of many talents."

We laughed. Courtney had asked him to play some classical music, and the missionaries thought it was a great idea.

Mother and I sat on the front row and I glanced around, looking for Dad. He was nowhere in sight. Mom knew I was looking for him, and she held my hand.

I closed my eyes, remembering the spiritual feeling I'd had so many times, when it almost seemed as if someone was trying to hug me.

The elders were about to begin the program, when suddenly, in walked Dad with Gloria. My chin dropped. Dad was wearing baptism whites!

"Dad?" I said, turning as white as my clothing.

He grinned, his eyes filling with tears. "This is the church I've been going to with Gloria," he said. "I've been taking the missionary lessons, too."

Gloria looked ready to burst with joy, and hugged me. "I'm so happy for you," she said. Then she introduced herself to Mother and they shook hands.

"Why didn't you tell me?" I asked Dad, jumping up to hug him.

"I didn't want it to influence your decision. You had to find out for yourself."

I beamed. This was cool. So that's why he wouldn't tell me his reason for giving me permission! "When did you get your answer?"

"Believe it or not," he said, "it was when I was talking to you on the phone. I guess I had known, but I'd been waiting for some big revelation or something. It turns out you were right; quiet certainty is an answer, too."

Now Mom stood up and gave Dad's arm a squeeze. "Congratulations," she said. "A double baptism."

"How about you?" Dad asked her. "You going to look into this?"

"Well," she said, smiling at Dad and Gloria, "Considering recent events, I'd say anything's possible."

Dad held us all then, and at last I felt what I'd been waiting for. The hug was complete.

About the Author

Joni Hilton is the popular author of numerous novels and nonfiction works for both LDS and national markets. She has a Master of Fine Arts degree in professional writing from the University of Southern California, and she frequently writes for several national magazines. She hosted her own daily television talk show for four years in Los Angeles. *That's What Friends Are For* was inspired by many of her experiences as a professional journalist, as a model, and as a former Miss California.

Next to mothering and writing, Joni enjoys creative cooking, and has won many state and national cook-offs. She and her husband, Bob, and their four children live in Sacramento, California.